PRAISE FOR
CATHERINE LANIGAN:

"Lanigan knows her genre well...."
—*Publishers Weekly*

"As a storyteller, Catherine Lanigan is in a class by herself." —*Affaire de Coeur*

"Catherine Lanigan's books...represent the changing—and booming—genre of women's fiction." —*Chicago Tribune*

"Catherine Lanigan will make you cheer and cry."
—*Romantic Times*

"Catherine Lanigan is a master storyteller."
—*Rave Reviews*

* * * * *

Catherine Lanigan is the bestselling author of the novelizations of the blockbuster movies *Romancing the Stone* and *The Jewel of the Nile.*

Dear Reader,

February, month of valentines, celebrates lovers—which is what Silhouette Desire does *every* month of the year. So this month, we have an extraspecial lineup of sensual and emotional page-turners. But how do you choose which exciting book to read first when all six stories are asking *Be Mine?*

Bestselling author Barbara Boswell delivers February's MAN OF THE MONTH, a gorgeous doctor who insists on being a full-time father to his newly discovered child, in *The Brennan Baby. Bride of the Bad Boy* is the wonderful first book in Elizabeth Bevarly's brand-new BLAME IT ON BOB trilogy. Don't miss this fun story about a marriage of inconvenience!

Cupid slings an arrow at neighboring ranchers in *Her Torrid Temporary Marriage* by Sara Orwig. Next, a woman's thirtieth-birthday wish brings her a supersexy cowboy—and an unexpected pregnancy—in *The Texan,* by Catherine Lanigan. Carole Buck brings red-hot chemistry to the pages of *Three-Alarm Love.* And Barbara McCauley's *Courtship in Granite Ridge* reunites a single mother with the man she'd always loved.

Have a romantic holiday this month—and every month—with Silhouette Desire. Enjoy!

Melissa Senate

Melissa Senate
Senior Editor

Please address questions and book requests to:
Silhouette Reader Service
U.S.: 3010 Walden Ave., P.O. Box 1325, Buffalo, NY 14269
Canadian: P.O. Box 609, Fort Erie, Ont. L2A 5X3

CATHERINE LANIGAN
THE TEXAN

SILHOUETTE *Desire*®

Published by Silhouette Books

America's Publisher of Contemporary Romance

SILHOUETTE BOOKS

ISBN 0-373-76126-0

THE TEXAN

Printed in U.S.A.

CATHERINE LANIGAN

As a college freshman, Catherine Lanigan was told by her creative-writing professor that she had no talent and would never earn a living as a writer. With ten best-selling romance novels and praise from *Affaire de Coeur*, calling her "an unequalled and simply fabulous storyteller," Catherine has proven him wrong in a very big way.

Catherine is also the bestselling author of the novelizations of the smash movies *Romancing the Stone* and *The Jewel of the Nile*. When not writing, she enjoys entertaining her friends with innovative gourmet meals.

For Charlotte Breeze and Karen Taylor Richman.
My thanks for all your hard work and plugging away
on this project long enough for serendipity to take
the credit.

Prologue

Houston, Texas

"**I** won't believe for a second that I'm finished," Rafe Whitten growled as he catapulted his six-foot-two-inch, wide-shouldered frame out of the brown leather chair in his accountant's office. "Defeat is not in my vocabulary, Matt. You of all people should know that."

Matt Leads instantly hung his head and shook it in frustration. "It's this 'die-hard' attitude of yours that's gotten you into this financial black hole, Rafe. Tele-Cept was your brainstorm and probably would have gone on forever. Embezzlement is not easily recoverable."

Raking his hand through his thick dark hair, Rafe placed his booted feet wide apart, folded his arms across his expansive chest and glared at Matt. "Don't I know it. But bankruptcy? Matt, I can't do it. It's not the Whitten way of doing business. My clients believe in me. I've made promises I must keep.''

Matt was only a year younger than his thirty-three-year-old friend, Rafe, but it was at times like these he felt as old as Methuselah and twice as wise. ''If you'd listened to me—''

''The ranch is all I have left,'' Rafe interrupted him. ''When my parents died they intended for me to keep it for their grandchildren.''

''Considering fatherhood is one of your least favorite topics, why are you letting the ranch and a bunch of horses keep you from making good at least the majority of this debt?''

Rafe ground his jaw and shoved his hands into his pockets. ''They're not just horses to me, Matt.''

''Sorry,'' Matt apologized. He knew how close Rafe was to his menagerie of horses, bulls, cats, dogs, ducks, birds and any other animal that was smart enough to recognize a sucker when it saw one. Matt knew from Rafe's receipts at the Waller County Feed stores that he would rather spend money on animal feed and grain than on food for himself.

''I've had a lot of dreams about that ranch, Matt. I always believed I'd make them come true. Now you're telling me it's impossible.''

''I never said that. Miracles happen every day. It's just that I've never seen any.'' Discernment narrowed Matt's brown eyes. ''Have you?''

Rafe immediately stopped pacing. ''No.''

Despite his resolve to banish his anger toward his former business associate, Paul Thomas, haunting visions of their college comradery bored deeply into Rafe's trusting heart. Letting even more blood over the situation was the fact that his five-year relationship with Cheryl Hudson had ended the day she walked out of his life to be with Paul. She'd left Rafe a note saying she couldn't wait forever till Rafe made his millions. She'd already wasted too much of her youth. She wanted to "live."

The fact that he'd given his heart to a gold digger hurt Rafe's pride, but not nearly as much as the knowledge that she'd never loved him in return. He'd been a fool.

More than anything Rafe hated the way his stomach still turned over every time he thought about Cheryl. Her betrayal had been so razor-sharp that he felt he'd been left for dead before he even knew he was cut. Paul's part in Rafe's annihilation was secondary, but it was easier for Rafe to talk about Paul than about Cheryl. At least his emotions didn't stick so viciously in his craw.

Rafe had learned all too well that the only way to fight anger and bitterness was to turn himself off…completely. Detachment was becoming a way of life for him and it suited him just fine. Nobody could ever hurt him again as long as he didn't allow it, he'd told himself.

Rafe turned cool blue eyes back to Matt. "What's done is done. I can't change the past. If you truly believe selling the ranch is the way I should go…"

"I do. There's a slim chance we won't have to declare bankruptcy."

"Bankruptcy is not an option for me. Few people realize it, but that black mark is made with indelible ink."

Rafe looked out the nineteenth-story window at the Houston skyline. Beyond downtown stretched miles of highways, out to a second skyline of buildings around the Galleria and then further out to the northwest where the sprawling city was no more than scattered pockets of houses. Where land and sky drew together on the horizon was his beloved ranch. His mouth went dry knowing he'd lost it.

How cocky he'd been just a year ago. He'd thought Houston sat squarely in the palm of his hand. Every top executive wanted to do business with him. His technology was on the cutting edge of the lightning-fast world of global telecommunications. Rafe Whitten was the "man to watch" the *Houston Chronicle* had written. Even the *Wall Street Journal* cited him for his clever deal-cutting. Money marketers and stockbrokers in every major city were salivating over the day he'd take his company public. He was going to be a multimillionaire overnight, or so everyone thought.

But his partner, Paul, had gotten too greedy, too soon. He not only blew the deal, he sold Rafe down the river while doing it. With the company coffers wiped out, Rafe owed his initial investors millions of dollars. He'd sold everything he owned, the townhouse inside the Loop, his cars, ski boat and the lake condo at Walden. This was worse than the oil crash less than a decade ago. He'd weathered that downturn despite the fact he'd only been twenty-six years old. This time, his situation was much worse; the bust came from a viper at home.

Matt could tell from the flinty look in Rafe's eyes that his friend was thinking about Cheryl.

Rafe's hollow voice broke the silence. "I should have listened to you, Matt. From the day I met that blond she-devil at the Houston Livestock and Rodeo Show, you told me she was bad news walking. I remember accusing you of being too cerebral, too analytical and maybe even a bit jealous. Being a good friend, you kept your mouth shut. For a while we were happy, though. The company was moving along slowly but steadily in the kind of way that makes you CPAs comfortable. I gave Cheryl enough trinkets to keep her amused. Obviously, it wasn't enough."

Matt stood and went over to Rafe, put his hand on his friend's shoulder. "I wish I'd been wrong about her."

"Me, too."

"You know, Rafe, we accountants like everything neat and tidy. So I hope you won't get mad at me if I ask you something."

His blue eyes, now reflecting a hard steel gray, never wavered from the horizon. "What is it?"

"Something here doesn't add up. You've never been gullible a moment in your life that I've ever seen. So how is it that someone with your brains and savvy fell for her tricks? It just doesn't seem right. There's a very large piece of this puzzle missing."

Rafe shrugged. "Hey, love is blind." He finally turned to Matt, but his eyes were colder than ever. "You can bet one thing. I'll never let any of it happen to me again. Once bitten..."

"You can't mean you intend to be alone forever."

"I don't see a problem with that. You see a problem?" Rafe asked angrily, a nerve along his jawline twitching.

"Gotcha," Matt replied quickly, not wanting to upset his friend anymore.

Turning to the brass hatrack, Rafe took his black cowboy hat off the top hook and settled it on his head. He put his hand out to Matt. "Thanks for all your help. You've been a good friend."

Feeling somehow guilty and responsible for Rafe's solemn mood, Matt said, "Why don't we go out for a drink before you head back to the ranch?"

"Naw. The last thing I want is to be around a bunch of people who..."

Frustrated with Rafe's seemingly implacable need to cut himself off from humanity, Matt interrupted. "Who might be having fun? Who might take your mind off things?'' Suddenly, Matt was on a mission. If he let Rafe drive home in his present mood, he would only retreat into a deeper depression. True, Rafe had good reasons to be gloomy, but he'd been telling Matt he was giving up on life. Thoughts that black had to be attacked before their stain set in permanently.

"I have things to do," Rafe replied, as he turned toward the door.

Matt caught him by the arm. "Well, I don't. Since I know you can't possibly pay me all you owe me, the least you can do is buy me a beer on my birthday."

"Aw, you're kidding. I didn't know it was your birthday. Of course we'll go out."

"Great!" Matt said grabbing his briefcase and shoving his arms in his jacket. "Actually, it's not my birthday," he confessed sheepishly as he held the office door for Rafe.

"Why, you little…" Rafe playfully raised his fist.

"Watch it. You're bigger than I am. It was only a little lie. Besides, today must be *somebody's* birthday."

"Look, Matt. I'll have a beer with you, but I'm not going to celebrate," Rafe said with finality as they left.

One

"**I**'m giving up men forever," Angela Morton sighed glumly to her friends and co-workers, Ilsa Prentiss and Julia Freeman. As Angela sank her chin into her hand, one of the black-and-silver "Over the Hill" balloons that was tied to the back of her chair bobbed up and down, hitting her in the face. She batted it away.

"This is supposed to be your thirtieth birthday party. It's time to have fun!" Ilsa replied with a wide smile.

"Don't be so hard on her," Julia scolded Ilsa, with her usual mother-hen tone of voice. Julia was the receptionist at the offices of Patrick Gallagher Realtors and being the oldest of the three at the ripe old age of thirty-two, she felt she was not only more experienced in "men matters," but she'd been married and divorced when both Angela and Ilsa had not been married at all…yet. She was confident her advice was always on target.

"Look at her," Ilsa said, pointing at Angela. "I've never seen a more perfect portrait of doom. The bags under her eyes are packed for Europe."

"What bags?" Angela asked and instantly looked under her chair for her purse. "Since when have I ever had bags? God! Getting old is the pits," she said, but Ilsa and Julia weren't listening. They were too busy dissecting Angela's life for her. "I've been working overtime lately. I'm trying to make a living," she replied with false haughtiness. "I would never waste a minute's sleep over a man. You can be sure of that."

"Certainly not," Ilsa commented as her eyes zeroed in on a tall, lean, blond cowboy in a very tight pair of jeans and a black hat. "Anyway, I overheard Randy barking orders at you last week to get your sales up."

"Don't remind me. Not on my birthday. Okay?"

"I think she's absolutely right to give up men," Julia said flatly as she took a long sip of a gigantic frozen margarita in front of her.

"You do?" Angela's eyes widened in shock. "Why?"

"Take a look at your track record. First was James. What a loser that guy was. He couldn't keep a job for more than six months. Once you finally kicked him out of the apartment, you discovered he'd maxed your cards."

"That was six years ago," Angela said.

"Yeah. And it took you eighteen months to pay off the bills. Then there was Rick who thought it was okay to hit on all your girlfriends."

"A real peach of a guy," Ilsa agreed, munching on her sixth handful of snack mix.

"Last but not least was Larry. The jerk of all jerks who not only married your college roommate, but screwed you out of at least six months of real estate commissions. Remember the rules? Never sleep with a Realtor.''

Angela was more depressed than ever. ''Let's not drag up the past, shall we?''

''We learn from the past,'' Julia wagged her finger at her friend.

''That is precisely what I'm talking about. Men today aren't *real* men like...my great-grandfather was.''

''Do we have to hear this story again?'' Julia frowned.

Ilsa cut her off. ''But it's so romantic. Tell us again, Angela.''

''He fell in love with my great-grandmother the first time he laid eyes on her at the Governor's Ball in New Orleans. He told her they would build a wonderful life together on his ranch west of San Antonio. She loved him, too, and married him the next month. She worked right alongside him every day of her life. They were never apart. Not even for a single night. Until the day they died, they were kind and considerate toward one another.''

''I do love this story,'' Ilsa sighed.

''Men today are afraid of commitment. Afraid of working. Afraid of children. Afraid to live. So, why should I waste my precious time on any of them?''

Julia munched on the piece of lime in her margarita. ''You have a point. However, this isn't 1895. This is the Post Oak Ranch. It's a bar. A meeting place. Not a real ranch, okay?''

''I'm not an idiot, you know,'' Angela sniffed.

''No, you're our best friend,'' Ilsa chimed in while giving Julia a stabbing look.

Julia's eyes filled with apology. ''I'm sorry. It's just that I want you to be happy. And I'm going to make up by finding you just the right dancing partner for tonight. Let's see,'' Julia's eyes scrupulously examined every unattached man. ''No, too old. That one is too cocky. And that blond, tall drink of water over there is…is…heading this way.''

"Oh, my God!'' Angela blushed, then smiled at the handsome man who smiled back at her. At least that was what it seemed like he was doing.

The man walked up to their table and put his arm on the back of Julia's chair. "Would you like to dance?'' he asked.

Julia's breath caught in her throat. "I— I—'' She looked at Angela who nodded back. "I'd love to.''

Not five seconds later a dark-haired younger man wearing jeans, a plaid shirt and tennis shoes asked Ilsa to dance.

Angela was alone at last, which was just the way she liked it. "Now I can daydream all I want without feeling guilty,'' she mumbled to herself as she let her mind wander.

She knew her friends meant well, but they simply didn't understand her. Glaringly aware of all her past mistakes, Angela resolved that on this birthday, the beginning of a new decade in her life, she would never, ever fall in love again, though she really didn't want to give up men all together.

If there ever was a "next time'' in her life, she would be sensible. She would test his motives and learn to be friends first and lovers later. Integrity and loyalty in a man counted for more than just sexual attraction. She would never again settle for anyone who wasn't the kind of man her great-grandfather had been.

"See? This isn't so bad, is it, Rafe?'' Matt asked as the bartender placed two long-necked beer bottles in front of them.

Rafe took a long draw on the beer as he looked around

the room. It was the usual mesh of working girls looking for a man to take care of them and the even more usual ogling businessmen who wanted to do the caring...but only for one night. "Nothing changes much, does it?" Rafe scoffed and turned back to the bar.

Just then, out of the corner of his eye, Rafe caught a glimpse of bobbing black-and-white balloons. "I don't believe it. It really *is* someone's birthday," he said with surprise.

Rafe was about to make another wisecrack when the softest pair of brown eyes set in the most ethereal face he'd ever seen looked straight at him.

His breath caught in his throat as her eyes settled on his face with a look of endearment he'd only previously seen in his mother's eyes. He couldn't tell if she was actually seeing him or looking through him. She didn't appear to mind that he was staring back. Neither smiling nor acknowledging his presence, her face shone with an inner peace he wished he'd cultivated for himself.

Looking rather out of place amid the harshly made-up women around her, the "birthday girl" as he mentally referred to her, wore little makeup and her blond hair fell in soft, natural waves down the sides of her heart-shaped ivory-pale face to her shoulders. He wanted to believe she used very little hair spray and certainly would never entertain the thought of having her hair "woven" with acrylic strands, the way Cheryl had. Women had millions of beauty secrets from fake eyelashes to plastic nails, silicone breasts and dyed, false hair to make them beautiful. Rafe wanted to believe that just this once, he'd found someone whose beauty was natural. Maybe it was possible this "birthday girl" could restore his faith.

Matt started to respond to Rafe's quip but stopped himself in time to watch his friend's decidedly strong reaction to the pretty blonde who looked as if this birthday would be the one to truly bury her. Matt couldn't figure out what held Rafe so spellbound. She wasn't half the ''looker'' type Rafe usually preferred and she looked so utterly… sad. Matt thought his friend needed a cheerleader to zap him out of his depressed state. A quick fling would do the trick, Matt thought. This girl was too much peaches and cream and too much of a real person.

Rafe slid his beer bottle onto the bar.

''Where you goin'?'' Matt asked.

''To celebrate someone's birthday,'' Rafe said without looking back at Matt.

Angela was unaware of the soft dreamy look on her face as she mused about her fantasy hero. He would be tall, strong and good-looking, but he would have a gentleman's manners and a code of ethics others would admire. He would be kind to children and animals. And when he spoke, he'd have a voice that sounded like…

''Happy birthday,'' a velvety, sensual voice poured over her.

Angela was so entranced by her own reveries, she thought she had imagined the voice. She stared blankly at the tall, handsome dark-haired man with flashing blue-gray eyes.

''Tell me I'm the first to dance with the birthday girl,'' he said.

''You are?'' Suddenly, Angela realized she was not dreaming. ''I mean, you *are!* Yes, I mean, I'd love to.''

His smile revealed perfectly white even teeth between full, sensual lips. His jawline was sharply hewn and his cheekbones were high as if he had Indian blood somewhere in his ancestry. His Western clothes were faded and snug on his lean, fit body.

Angela stood very close to him when she rose from her chair. She couldn't help detecting the faint smell of leather, as if he'd ridden into town on his horse. She would have swooned, but modern women didn't do such things.

His touch was gentle yet possessive as he took her hand and led the way through the crowd around the dance floor. It wasn't until she was behind him that she noticed his massively wide shoulders and chest that looked as if he could carry the weight of the world on them. Surely, he was a man of great responsibility. *He's my kind of man.*

Whoa! Slow down, Angela, she thought to herself. Get a grip, girl. He's only asked you to dance.

Melancholy strains of the country-western song being played filled the room as couples clung to each other under the dim colored lights. Angela wished she'd paid more attention to Ilsa's dance instructions, but the truth of the matter was that Angela was the first to volunteer for overtime and the last to frequent the clubs with her friends. The result was that she did not follow well. Nor did she line-dance or square-dance. None of that mattered because this man, who seemingly had walked out of her dreams and now held her body in a forceful yet graceful manner, had actually made her feel as if they were one of those dance teams in an old Ginger Rogers and Fred Astaire movie.

"Do you think we fit well?" he asked with that maddeningly sensual voice.

"I'm not sure," she replied coolly, wanting to prove to herself she was over men forever. This killer-looking hunk was not going to foul her newly planted resolution. If she could resist him, she could do anything.

The logical side of Angela's personality was quite pleased with her performance, but it was her romantic and heretofore overly impetuous side that shouted: *You idiot! Why don't you tell him what you're really feeling? Other girls would already have him wanting to take them home to bed.* "I mean, I think we fit fine." *That's being assertive? Angela, girl, no wonder you never get a real man.*

His breath was like a lover's caress on her neck. His hands were callused and no matter how she fought it, another image of him, on horseback, streaked across her mind. His chest was rock-hard and as she pressed her fingers into the tight muscles in his shoulders she could feel her body responding to him. She couldn't help leaning into him a bit more.

His hand slipped from the middle of her back to her waist and with splayed fingers, he pressed her body to his. Then he began moving his hips in rhythm to the music.

All this time, she'd thought he was coming on to her, but instead he was showing her what it was like to feel the music with her body. It was an incredible experience. He taught her how to catch the melody with her head and translate it into body language. They glided, swayed, turned and dipped according to the beat, the pulse and soul of the music. When the crescendo exploded, he spun Angela around so many times she was dizzy. She lost eye contact with the people around the dance floor as the room seemed to disappear. In order not to lose her balance, she was forced to lean against him. She looked in his eyes.

He gazed at her with smoky blue pools that seemed to promise eternity.

Quit, Angela! Wasn't it only moments ago you promised yourself not to ever fall under a man's spell again?

That's right, she thought. From now on she was going to be adult about all her relationships. She tried to look away from him, but his feet quick-stepped around hers so fast that she was no longer aware of touching the ground. She'd taken flight and he was the pilot.

The music fluttered into a second chorus and the tempo eased them back to gentler movements.

"And what's the birthday girl's name?" he asked, placing his slightly rough cheek against hers.

"Angela Morton," she replied haltingly. It was tough pretending her heaving lungs and banging heart were from the exuberant dance and not from him. After all, she wasn't affected by men anymore.

"Nice name," he whispered. "You feel like an angel." He hadn't meant to say that aloud, he thought. Rafe had to shake his head to dispel the romantic images from his brain. What was he thinking?

God, I don't think I can stand this much longer. He's doing everything right! He would have to call her "angel," just like her father and grandfather had. Not one person she'd ever dated had figured that much out.

"I do?" she asked.

"Yes. Soft. Sweet and very, very warm." He pressed his hand against her back again.

Her vow of becoming friends first and lovers later was becoming a dim memory as her breasts pressed against his granite chest. She didn't like the fact that her breasts were far too sensitive for her own good. She couldn't help but imagine what it would be like for him to touch her delicate skin. She squeezed her eyes closed, hoping the thought would disappear.

"What's wrong?" he asked.

"Nothing." *Everything's wrong. I'm responding to him more than any man in my entire life. I wish to heaven there was something I didn't like about him.*

"You closed your eyes so tightly, I thought maybe you'd lost your contact or something."

"I don't wear contacts."

"I was holding you too tightly then?" he asked, putting his hand up to her chin and lifting her face to his. "I've been accused of getting carried away when I dance. It's just that I'm a sucker for these torchy ballads. I've always liked music I could understand the words to…sing to."

Angela felt her mouth go dry. *Wouldn't you know it? Just my luck he likes the same music I do. I'll find something wrong with him yet. After all, nobody's perfect.* "Country-western is too whiny for me. I like real oldies…like Cole Porter." *I'll bet he's never heard of Cole Porter or Gershwin for that matter.*

"Where did you come from? The stars? I've always thought no song will ever top 'Night and Day,'" he replied, flabbergasted.

Angela gulped. She'd never met anyone who liked her music. "I would have thought you were the George Strait type."

"Honky-tonk bars and good-time lovers?"

"Yes," she said feeling oddly nervous about his caustic reply.

"I'm that, too."

I thought so. Angela dragged her eyes away from his cool, steady gaze and pretended his honest answer was just fine with her. The last thing she needed was a cavalier cowboy who racked up affairs like notches on a gunbelt.

They danced silently for what seemed like an eternity before Rafe broke the tension by asking her where she worked.

"I'm a Realtor. My office is on San Felipe, so it's not far to my townhouse," she replied, looking up at him and forcing herself to feign the same aloofness he'd injected into his voice.

Without warning, he kissed her.

An unbelievable fire leapt through her body the instant their lips touched. He held nothing back and claimed her mouth with such raw passion, she wondered how she'd survive the intensity.

His arms pulled and pressed her body into his, though they undulated to the music. Breast to chest, belly to belly and with his pelvis crushing into hers, her dream man locked his body to hers. Wonderfully, she felt as if she were melting into him. There was such a possessiveness about his kiss that she felt as if she was precious to him. Never had she felt so close to anyone. His kiss was magic. His lips were not hard or unrelenting, nor were they too soft, lacking purpose. His kiss was the kiss she'd imagined in her dreams all her life. He tasted divine, she thought as his lips slanted over her mouth. His tongue traced the edge of her mouth and then prodded her lips apart stroking the interior. She matched his low, sexual moan of surrender with one of her own. She thought she could almost feel their hearts entwine.

She breathed in his breath. She tasted his warm juices as she buried her hand in his nape. She could never allow this kiss to end. This was heaven. This was the feeling she'd always dreamed of, but never dared to admit to anyone, not even to herself.

He showed no sign of wanting to stop. Instead, his tongue probed more deeply, sending rivers of chills cascading over the hills and valleys of her body. Torrid blasts of desire mercifully extinguished the chills. As perspiration broke out between her breasts and between her legs, she felt herself begin to move to the rhythm of the hypnotic melody he was creating within her. She could no longer hear the sad refrain from the stereo system. She was listening with her heart. She could only hope he was hearing the same song.

Slamming, pounding against her rib cage, her heart told her that she'd never been this alive. The heat of his body matched hers degree for degree. His breath came in the same halting pants as hers. They were in sync with every nerve in their bodies. Angela knew that she would never again find anyone to thrill her so much with just a kiss.

Hearing nothing but the ancient crescendo their bodies played, Angela was unaware the music had ended. A rock tune began; its only purpose was to break lovers apart.

Reluctantly, his tongue bowed out of the dance with hers. His lips pressed her mouth with tiny remembrances of the passion they'd shared. Whirling through the galaxy, Angela found her return to reality jolting.

"Thank you for the dance," she whispered pressing her forehead next to his as they gazed at each other.

"I hope your birthday kiss met your expectations," he replied with husky tones.

"It was beyond belief."

"Good. Then I'll return you to your friends."

Angela felt as if she'd been dashed with icy water. Her legs were still half numb, though she forced them to move off the dance floor. She blinked twice trying to remember where she was and what she was doing here. This was a dream. He was her dream man. Magic like this only happened in dreams. Her dreams especially.

Then she remembered Julia and Ilsa. They were still on the dance floor and hadn't seen what had happened.

He held the chair for her again as she sat down and smiled up at him. She touched his hand. *He's real! I'm doomed!* She sighed. *I suppose there's some solace in the fact that I haven't gone crazy.*

"Won't you stay and meet my friends?" she asked.

He shook his head. His smoky blue eyes had changed color again—now they were steel gray. Somehow, he looked like a stranger. "I can't. I have a prior commitment." He kissed the top of her head. "Sorry."

Without another word he walked back to the bar, where he was met by another man dressed in a business suit. Angela couldn't believe it. The man of her dreams had walked into and out of her life and she didn't even know his name.

Matt's startled expression didn't deter Rafe from his purposeful dash to the exit. "Where are you going?"

"Home."

"Are you nuts? She liked you. I could have sworn you liked her, judging from that kiss," Matt said as he followed quickly behind.

"So?"

"So maybe she's just what you need to snap you out of your depression."

Rafe pushed the door open with the flats of both palms. "I am *not* depressed. I'm being smart."

Matt pulled up short as Rafe came to a sudden stop. "Look, you can't go around letting one bad experience dictate the rest of your life. Besides, this girl looked kinda sweet. Like a—"

"She's a Realtor, is all."

Matt noticed Rafe was beginning to calm down as he talked. "What's her name?"

"Angela Morton." Rafe dug in his jeans pocket for his truck keys. "I gotta get back. Feed the horses, you know."

Matt glanced back at the entrance doors. "Have one more beer."

"No, Matt." Rafe's eyes narrowed to icy slits as he started toward his truck.

In exasperation, Matt yelled after his friend. "She was an angel. What's the matter with you?"

Without looking back Rafe muttered, "Temporary insanity."

Two

Nestled at the far end of Post Oak Lane beneath the shadow of the twenty-seven-story One Riverway building, a group of elegant, cosmopolitan townhomes had been built during the oil-boom days of the late seventies and early eighties.

As Angela hit the automatic garage door button and drove her BMW inside, she remembered the day she bought her home. She'd only been twenty-six years old when she'd discovered this building, with its open and spacious floor plan. It had been about to go into foreclosure. Though the Houston real estate market had been in the doldrums back in 1992, Angela believed enough in her own abilities and talents to know that, no matter what, she would always make the mortgage payment. Having saved the bulk of her commissions ever since she'd graduated from University of Texas with a business degree, she had not only negotiated the price to thirty thousand dollars below the appraisal value, she'd used just half her savings for the down payment, keeping the rest in U.S. Treasury bills. She knew that the overpriced homes in that area would never appreciate, and if she ever did eventually break even on her investment it would be due solely to her negotiating skill. She had also believed that living in a safe neighborhood less than ten minutes from her office was peace of mind money could never buy.

At the time, Julia, Ilsa and every other person with whom she'd had even the briefest encounter thought she was nuts. Four years later she'd not only moved the last of her family heirlooms out of storage, had them refinished and reconstructed, but she'd created a nostalgic blend of Old West and an early 1920s "prairie" look that suddenly was now all the rage.

Though the sweeping circular staircase might have seemed out of place with her Navajo rugs, chandelier, dark brown leather club chairs and off-white-cotton-slip-covered sofas, she redeemed it by ripping up the old white carpeting and installing honey-colored wood steps to match the same-hued wood on the first floor.

She remembered the two-story ranch house her great-grandfather, Daniel, had built for her great-grandmother, Evelyn. The open prairie had been a stark contrast to Evelyn's extravagant surroundings in New Orleans. She'd let Daniel have his way with nearly all the house designs, except for the staircase. She'd told him from the day they were married in 1885 that she intended that he wait for her at the bottom of the stairs every evening before dinner, because she wanted to see his face light up the way it had when she'd walked down the aisle at their wedding. The staircase was his wedding gift to her.

Angela was the first Morton in generations to move out of that house. At the tender age of eighteen, she had lost both her parents in a private plane crash near Ruidosa, and had suddenly found herself responsible for not only all the funeral arrangements and the will, but also for a large mortgage that her father had taken out on the house to keep the cattle ranch going "until things turned around." Angela realized she would have to sell the ranch.

Sentimentally attached to every rock, tree, bird and bush on the property, and to every brick and board of the house, Angela cried for weeks over the prospect of losing her family home. However, once she understood that her future depended on no one but herself, she slipped out of her teens and into adulthood overnight. She listed the house herself, showed it to every prospective buyer and negotiated the final sale. Without a backward glance she packed everything down to the last dish, and put it all in storage to wait until she had finished college and built or bought a house of her own.

It took her nine years to build up the capital she needed and in the process she developed a credible reputation as a Realtor in the nation's fourth-largest city. Nothing had come easily to Angela but she'd always had twice the determination and drive of her colleagues, and certainly more than her competitors. She was proud of her home and her accomplishments.

Awkwardly loaded down with birthday gifts, mementos, balloons and bows, Angela entered the blue-and-white country kitchen. She leaned over and dumped her belongings on the kitchen counter. Glancing at her phone recorder she saw that the red light was steady. There had been no calls.

Walking into the foyer, Angela found her hundred-and-ten-pound pedigreed six-year-old golden retriever, Rebel, sitting on the third step of the winding staircase happily panting in anticipation of his usual bear hug.

"Hiya, fella," Angela greeted him, putting her face next to his. Rebel licked the tip of her nose. "Oh, thank you for my kisses. Mommy likes those kisses." She patted his head. "You had to wait up a long time for me tonight, didn't you? Well, I really appreciate it," she said hugging him again.

Rebel kissed her face again and she laughed at him.

"Was that my birthday kiss?" she asked. Suddenly, she heard her own voice turn hollow and empty.

I've already gotten my birthday kiss, but I don't know his name. I don't know anything about him except that he wasn't as impressed with me as I was with him.

How very odd that this year she'd dreaded her birthday. Julia had wanted to chalk up her depression to ticking biological clocks and all that sort of thing, but Angela liked to think she was being practical. For the first time since college her birthday would not revolve around the breaking-up, making-up, or getting-over-it stage of another rotten relationship. This year she could honestly say she was "man-free." She'd kicked the habit of rushing into yet another love affair in which she did most of the loving.

In the past year or so Angela's greatest revelation had been that she'd always settled for less than Mr. Perfect because she'd felt alone ever since her parents died. She missed them greatly, but nothing could ever bring them back to life. Now she was in the process of teaching herself how to keep their memories alive, yet still continue on with her own life.

Being honest with herself, she had to admit that she liked the peace and serenity of being without a demanding relationship. She didn't particularly want or need a man.

With a wide circle of friends and co-workers who included her in their family traditions, Angela knew how to get through family holidays without a family. She wasn't the least bit lonely.

The prospect of attending the upcoming holiday office parties and dinners without a date did not daunt her. She'd spent far too many Christmases having her illusions shattered by boyfriends who turned out to be nothing special at all.

"Then *you* had to show up!" she exclaimed, flinging her arms in the air.

Rising from the steps, she went into the living room and flopped on the new white-slipcovered antique sofa she'd had refurbished for the holidays. She crooked her arm over her eyes hoping to wipe out the vision of her dream man's face. She could still feel the warmth of his arms and hear his heartbeat. He wasn't a dream. If anything he was alarmingly real. His presence poked holes in every single one of her resolutions. He had made her want someone special in her life, just as her mother had told her she would.

Angela's parents' marriage was one of those incredible romantic flings that old Cary Grant movies depicted, except that their marriage had lasted over twenty years before they died. Perhaps if her parents had divorced, like nearly everyone else in the country, then Angela could at least have blamed her inability to choose the proper mate on her parents' bad example.

Doomed to believe in true love practically since her first breath, Angela had finally come to understand that her trust in her fellow man was misplaced. The rest of the world was not kind to people like herself. It was too easy for her to be taken advantage of, duped and left broken-hearted. However, Angela had decided years ago she was not the cynical type, like Julia, even though Julia seemed to get through problems with greater ease. Angela's only defense was to elect to leave the rest of the world to its own devices.

Her plan for the future had nearly worked.

This is all so silly. I don't even know his name. Or where he lives or works. He only knows I'm a Realtor like hundreds of other women in this city. Crooking her arms behind her head she stared at the ceiling. *And what was all that about a "prior commitment," anyway? Probably some Heather Locklear look-alike with a Ph.D.!*

Sullenly, she rose from the sofa, stepped over Rebel who was sleeping on the floor in the foyer, and went up the stairs.

She turned on the light in her bedroom, a mix of her mother's beautiful Southern antiques and her grandmother's delicate handmade lace spreads and bed linens. Crossing the room she stopped at the gilded French mirror that had once belonged to her great-grandmother.

Looking deeply into the reflection of her brown eyes she was surprised to see tears forming. Silently, the tears dropped straight to the vanity, not marking her cheeks. Angela knew why they were falling.

I'm the only one who will ever know what really happened to me tonight, she thought, turning toward her closet where she hung up her clothes.

The house held a chill that night, as gusty winds brought a cold front. Sleeping under a down comforter was a luxury in subtropical Houston. This was just the kind of night meant for snuggling, she thought as she crawled between the sheets.

"Julia is right, as usual," she said aloud to herself. "I have exaggerated this whole thing. It was just a dance. Just a kiss. Nothing more."

If it was only a kiss, then why can't I forget his kiss like I have so many others? Why were his lips so divine that their touch has somehow wiped out the memory of every other man's lips? If our meeting was so darned insignificant, then why can I still hear the particular sweet sound of his voice? Why can I still smell him as if he were lying here in this bed with me? Why is he haunting me like this?

Angela thought she could see his eyes looking at her, flashing like blue crystals in the night, seeking her out in the darkness. As if she were still wrapped in his arms, she could feel the tension in his muscles, still hear the soft sound of his breath as he placed his lips next to her ear. How was it possible to continue experiencing him as if he'd never left her?

Many times Angela had met a man and come home feeling as if she could dance on the ceiling, but there had always been signals telling her that something was not quite right. Maybe she'd forgotten the color of his eyes even on the fourth date. She couldn't remember his name or where he worked. She didn't like the cut of his clothes or the thousand and one bad habits or bad manners Tom or Allan or Sid had displayed. There had always been some tiny "thing" she'd convinced herself she would have to abide in order to make this or that relationship "work."

But this man tonight was different. For the life of her she resisted saying those corny things she'd read in novels or heard in dialogue on the soap operas. Angela didn't believe in soul mates or destiny. She believed in being practical with her life. For months she'd been hell-bent on raising self-reliance to an art form. Suddenly, she found herself wanting someone.

It's just the romance of the holidays that is making me think this way. Feel this way.

She hugged herself and pulled the comforter to her neck. She was just fine within the cocoon of the life she'd created for herself. She didn't need dream heroes walking in and messing up everything.

Besides, there was no such thing as a modern-day hero. The last of them had lived nearly a hundred years ago when her great-grandfather had lived in West Texas.

The man she'd met and danced with tonight would undoubtedly never think about her again. It was only right that she should banish him from her mind as well.

Confident she would awaken in the morning with only the faintest memory of her birthday kiss, Angela closed her eyes.

In minutes Angela slipped easily into sleep as her mystery man walked boldly into her dream.

Three

Angela walked out of the weekly staff meeting feeling like five pounds of dog meat. "Does Randy always have to pick on me?"

"Right now, you're the only one screwing up. This isn't like you, Angela. Last year, you were number one in the company and one of the top twenty-five producers in Houston. Then six months ago, your numbers started falling. Sometimes I think you've taken this birthday thing too much to heart."

It's not being thirty that bothers me. It's finding out there's no such thing as a "hero" anymore. "It's an inner-growth thing, Julia. Don't worry about it." *I'll look for a group workshop for "fairy-tale junkies."*

Julia put her hand on Angela's shoulder and pulled her aside. "I'm only saying this for your own good. Randy's right. Sales haven't been this good in Houston since the oil crash. We're all making money and you're not. The problem is only with you, sugar. Maybe if you'd get that damn mystery cowboy out of your head, you'd..."

Feigning ignorance, Angela tossed her arms in the air. "I haven't the slightest idea what you mean."

Julia leaned over conspiratorially as a trio of their fellow agents passed by. "I know guys like him, Angela. They breeze into your life, make you think you hung the moon and then whammo! You never see or hear from them again. You don't even know his name. So forget him."

"I will. I mean, I did," Angela replied quickly, but from the quelling look in Julia's eyes she knew she wasn't fooling anyone. "I'm working the phones all this week. I even signed up for the graveyard shift on Sunday. How's that?"

Julia shook her head. "I know it sounds as if I'm criticizing, but I'm just worried about you, is all. Besides, if you don't make some vacation money how can we plan our February trip to Grand Cayman, huh?" she asked jovially.

Nodding, Angela smiled. "I came to the same conclusion myself, Julia. I can do anything once I put my mind to it."

Just then Angela heard her name announced on the office PA system. "I've got a call. Maybe things are turning around already," she said, rushing to her desk.

She lifted the phone. "Angela Morton."

"This is Matt Leads. I'm a CPA and I got your name through an associate of mine. I was hoping you could help me out."

"I'll do my best, Mr. Leads."

Matt went on to explain that through a series of misfortunes one of his clients had been forced into bankruptcy. Since Matt would be handling the sale of the property, Matt requested that Angela fax their company's contract to him immediately. Then he asked if she could ride out to Waller County and take a look at the horse ranch and give him her professional assessment of what she felt it was worth. Matt wanted the property listed as quickly as possible.

"You realize that December is just about the worst time of year to sell, Mr. Leads."

"I understand. However, I personally plan to advertise the ranch in several upscale magazines along the East Coast. Texas always looks appealing to someone caught in the middle of a blizzard," he chuckled.

"I absolutely agree, Mr. Leads." Thrilled as she was, Angela kept her tone professional as she noted down the particulars of the property.

"Could you take a drive out there this afternoon? I'll let the owner know you're coming," Matt asked.

"Certainly. I'll prepare this paperwork and I can be there shortly in the early afternoon. Say, one o'clock?"

"That'll be fine," Matt replied and hung up.

Angela didn't waste a minute faxing the contracts to Matt Leads. She would need the owner's approval, of course, but she was confident she was turning her life around.

Obliterating the memory of an angel-faced birthday girl required superhuman strength and massive outputs of energy, but Rafe had infinite stores of both. In the week since his brief but unsettling interlude with Angela Morton, Rafe had put two coats of white paint on the ranch house, mended the corral fence, swept every last autumn leaf from the three acres surrounding the house and horse barn on his riding mower and restocked the enormous pond with bass. He'd pitched hay, bathed and brushed all eight of his horses, soaped his saddles and bridles and done just about everything he could to exhaust himself.

He forced himself to remember the incredibly painful wounds his ex-fiancée, Cheryl, had inflicted. He rehashed how easily he'd trusted her and given his love to her, and how she'd made a fool of him. Never again would he allow himself to be put in that position. He'd been a lot of things in his life, but never a fool, he thought as he rammed his pitchfork into a mound of fresh hay. He spread out the hay on the floor of Rising Star's stall.

Angela had seemed sweet, but then so had Cheryl in the beginning. Angela's kisses had been like nothing he'd ever experienced. He'd known passion, tenderness, lust and fun sex, but Angela was different. When he'd kissed her it was as if he'd kissed her before, he didn't know where or when. It was as if they'd had some kind of inner connection. Every move she'd made, even the most infinitesimal press of her lips against his had seemed familiar.

But that was impossible, he thought, stripping off his sweat-soaked plaid cotton shirt. He ground his jaw in frustration at himself. He should have been able to forget Angela. No one knew better than he that women were poison. Maybe if he repeated that to himself a thousand times he'd wise up.

Matt heard the blasting jangle of the horse-barn phone. Dropping the pitchfork and yanking a blue bandanna from his back jeans pocket to wipe the sweat from his face, Rafe picked up the phone. "Hey, Matt, how's it goin'?"

Rafe listened resignedly as Matt explained that he'd contracted with a Realtor to list the ranch. Though he'd been preparing the house for sale, it was still a blow to know he was going to lose his great-grandfather's land. "The company's sending an agent around one? It's almost that now." Rafe glanced out the barn door and saw a baby blue BMW convertible pull up to the ranch house. The car door opened.

"I think the Realtor is here." Rafe nearly dropped the phone when he saw Angela get out of the car. "Matt, you SOB!"

Matt chuckled with satisfaction. "I've never known you to react like that to a woman, Rafe. Maybe she's what the doctor ordered."

Rafe slammed down the receiver and stomped out of the horse barn. Rising Star whinnied approvingly as he sauntered into his freshly made-up stall.

Shielding her eyes from the bright afternoon sun, Angela surveyed the property. Thick clusters of oak trees still bearing half their leaves cast long wintry shadows over the newly painted ranch house. She couldn't help thinking this was just the sort of house she would have built had she been born a hundred years earlier. It had a wide wraparound front porch with delicate gingerbread trim along the roof line. Huge Boston ferns hung between the hand-carved posts and pots of winter chrysanthemums decorated the front steps. Though only two wicker rocking chairs sat on the back porch nearest the door to the kitchen, she imagined wicker tables and chairs, covered in summer calico, ready for huge family reunions.

The dark green shingled roof and green shutters made the house look as if it were part of its natural surroundings. Angela couldn't help smiling as she thought of the caption she could use to sell this ranch: "What home should be."

From a distance, Rafe's voice boomed across the corral and stretch of land like rolling tumbleweed. "There's been a big mistake. You might as well leave."

Mistake? Leave? Blasphemous words such as those she was hearing were not part of Angela's professional vocabulary. She didn't know who this Rafe Whitten was, but she wasn't moving a single inch until she'd appraised this property.

Who was this truculent oaf, who dared to stand between her and a sizable commission, judging by the extent of land and the excellent condition of the house and horse barn. Whirling around to face him, Angela stopped cold. "You?"

Rafe covered the remaining distance between them in three strides. His chest was heaving as much from rage at Matt as from physical exertion. Though it was the first of December, it was over seventy degrees and he'd been hard at work since dawn. Sweat poured from the top of his head down the sides of his face and dropped onto his tan shoulders and chest. He didn't realize every muscle in his body was corded making him look as if he could tear the house down singlehandedly. "I'm Rafe Whitten. It seems my friend, Matt Leads, has mingled in my affairs once too often. I'm sorry to have put you to this trouble, Angela."

A bit dizzy from the nearness of Rafe's half-naked body and becoming just as aggravated as he at being the butt of Matt's joke, Angela wanted to explode. Instead, for the first time in months she kept her wits about her. Though she would have given the world right then to throw herself into his unsuspecting arms and kiss the living daylights out of him, she only smiled calmly. "Matt Leads was the one waiting for you at the bar after you danced with me?"

"Yes," Rafe replied, with a curious look in his eyes.

"Your ranch house and all this property are to be sold. Correct?"

"Yes, but…"

"And Matt is acting in your behalf to dispose of this land due to your bankruptcy?"

"Yes."

"Then I'm not leaving."

"I don't want you to be my real estate agent," Rafe said flatly.

Angela's eyes narrowed. Hardball was one of her favorite games. "Are you discriminating against me because I'm a woman? Have I in any way conducted myself unprofessionally in our dealings thus far?"

Taken aback, Rafe replied, "Well, no."

"Then let's get something straight, Mr. Whitten. You and I shared a birthday kiss in a public place on a dance floor viewed by over a hundred people. I have attached no importance to it and neither should you."

Surprised, Rafe sucked in his breath as she continued.

"My firm has contracted with your representative to list this property. I can guarantee I will do a better job for you than any other Realtor in this city for one reason, and one reason alone. I have a reputation for keeping my mouth shut."

"What does that mean?"

"It means that if news of your bankruptcy were to leak out anywhere in this city, it would spread like wildfire not only in real estate, but other circles as well. People would think you must be desperate to dump this lovely home at fire-sale prices. We don't want that. We want to get you every dollar you deserve for preserving its inherent beauty and tradition. I believe we can get you the right price, and we can also sell the property in a relatively short period of time—no more than three months—and at this time of year that's considered rather fast. Not only that, when we do find a buyer, they will be the kind of people you'd like to invite for Sunday dinner." She clasped her hands behind her back and rocked a bit cockily back on her heels.

His blue-gray eyes flashed merrily. "You're damned good at what you do, aren't you, Miss Morton?"

Angela didn't miss the fact he'd dropped the familiarity of her first name. He was making a point. Well, so was she. "Yes, sir. I am."

He stuck out his hand to her. "Then you have a deal."

Angela shook his hand. Just as before, she felt a charge of electricity jolt through her body. She wished to heaven she didn't have to look in his eyes ever again. She wished she'd had the good sense to drive away when he told her to leave, but she hadn't. She needed this listing. She needed to make the sale and redeem herself in her boss's eyes. More important, she wanted to prove to herself she could be just as detached from him as he appeared to be from her.

He bowed slightly, his washboard stomach rippling as he did, and gave her a mocking smile. "Then may I suggest I show you the interior, Miss Morton?"

"Fine. We'll start with the kitchen," she replied following him. *He thinks he's irresistible, with that cute apple-shaped butt, twisted steel arms and back, and that come-hither smile. The only thing is, none of it will do him any good, unless a lady is willing. Fortunately, this lady's done that, been there, bought that T-shirt.*

Angela was in the game now, deeper than ever. But this time she was prepared.

Four

"The house was built by my great-grandfather in 1850, the year of the Great Compromise," Rafe said breezily as he showed Angela the original kitchen cabinets and cupboards that he'd painstakingly oiled since he was a child, as had his father before him. He explained that all the solid brass hardware was original, as were the cypresswood floors, mahogany-interior doors and trim. Nothing had been changed or added except the appliances and the granite countertops he'd installed five years ago.

"I hadn't expected to see anything quite this expensive or well done," Angela said.

"I had more money than sense back then, I guess."

Angela investigated the climate-controlled wine cellar with its rustic wooden crisscrossed racks. Rafe explained that his great-grandfather had built the room half below ground to ensure a cool climate for his homemade wines. It wasn't until Rafe's father, Michael, installed a modern cooling system in 1970 that their wines had been properly preserved.

"You've got wines that old?"

"Yes," he replied stiffly. "But some things are not for sale."

As Angela toured the rest of the house, she realized how bitter Rafe's words had been. Almost every room was completely bare of furnishings. Corners of rooms, where unfaded rugs met dark stained, untrodden wood, revealed the places where treasured family heirlooms had rested for nearly a hundred and fifty years...until now.

How devastating all this must be for him, she thought. To know that three generations had gone before him never losing, always gaining ground. Rafe was being forced to sell furnishings, china, silver and leatherbound books to settle a bankruptcy. Angela couldn't help thinking she wished there was some other, saner way for someone in his position to recover his losses. Unfortunately, she knew of none.

She followed him up the stairs to the second floor noticing the runner had been removed. "What color was the stair carpet?" she asked, simply for herself, so that she could better visualize how it had looked a hundred years ago.

"Royal blue and gold. Persian. My grandfather bought it in Tabriz from a trader. He said the blue was the color of my grandmother's eyes."

Thinking she'd never heard anything more dear or poetic, she felt her resolve toward Rafe melting with every word he spoke.

The bedrooms were larger than she'd imagined and the ceilings were higher, which would help bring a substantial price. Only the master bedroom still contained the original furniture. The antique mahogany rice bed nearly took Angela's breath away. She walked toward it with an out-stretched hand, as if she were being pulled into another century. "He gave this to her, didn't he?"

"My grandfather?" Rafe asked dispassionately. "Yes. Nearly everything of value was his. But I've adopted his philosophy."

Angela touched the delicate handmade lace canopy, thinking it felt lighter than an angel's wing. "Which is?"

"Things are meaningless..." He stopped in mid-sentence as Angela raised her face to him. At that moment she had that same faraway soft look in her eyes as she'd had the night they'd met. He didn't know what it was about her when she looked at him like that, but it was compelling and he thought he would lose his mind if he didn't touch her, hold her, kiss her...just one more time.

She hadn't realized he'd moved so close and when she looked up at him she was still thinking about the people who'd made love in this bed, creating their children and preserving their family for the future. She was unprepared for the touch of his hand against her cheek.

With his thumb he brushed away a lone tear that fell from her eye. "You're crying," he said, without asking for an explanation. "I know why. Every time I walk into this room, I can feel the enormity of loneliness in the world. You feel it, too, don't you?"

"Yes," she answered. How could he feel her spirit so effortlessly?

He kissed her delicately as if she were the most fragile of porcelains. He cupped her face with his strong, callused hands making it impossible for her to turn away from him. Logical thoughts loomed in a faraway distance, but they had no place in this world of emotion and overpowering physical passion. Rafe was responding just as eagerly to her. How was it he could be so utterly cold one moment and then instantly transform into this inferno of desire? Which was the real side of Rafe Whitten?

Angela placed her hands tenderly over his. She knew she should push him away and keep their discussion on the business at hand. But all she knew was that if she didn't let herself experience this man right here, right now, she might regret it for the rest of her life.

Never before had Angela abandoned herself to a man she barely knew, much less one she knew in her heart didn't want her. Though Rafe Whitten was moved by the moment, remembering a family who'd obviously left him as alone in the world as she was, her mind told her that when the kiss was over she would never feel his lips on hers again. He'd tell her that he regretted his impulsiveness; that he didn't want to get or be "involved" or "committed" to anyone. Angela had heard those words from men all her life. She'd never understood what it was about her that frightened them away. Perhaps in some deep way, she pushed them away, her inner self always knowing that none of them had truly been the right one.

Angela would be kind when he wanted to back away because she knew, as always, it would be for the best.

But for right now, it was as if they were suspended between time and space, hung in a netherworld of ghosts and dreams where the past met the present.

It wasn't curiosity that caused her to open her eyes, but a yearning to have more of him. As if reading her thoughts, slowly he opened his eyes at the same time. It was the first time she'd see him without his icy self-protective shields. His eyes were like crystal blue ponds and as she dove into him, she began to understand what it was like to touch someone's soul.

"Angel..." he breathed her name like a prayer and

before he could finish, his mouth had fallen upon hers like a penitent sinner asking forgiveness.

There was none of the masterful expertise she remembered from their night on the dance floor. This kiss was equally thrilling, but as he opened his lips wider and allowed her tongue inside him, she felt an equality between them.

Suddenly, he clasped his arms around her and pulled her into his naked chest. Angela's arms closed around him gently at first and then held him protectively within the circle of her love. She could tell he was as eager as she and as filled with desire, but something more frightening was happening to her. As profound as the moment was and as sublimely moved as she felt, she couldn't absolutely be sure he was feeling it as deeply as she.

Rafe's kiss grew rapacious as he slanted his mouth over hers again and again, demanding she give more of herself to him. Clutching her face between his hands he then slid his fingers up to her temples and into her hair keeping her prisoner. She could feel his heart slamming violently against his chest as if fighting for release. His body heat reached torrid temperatures as it radiated from his body into hers. She knew he was about to explode like a volcano. With a single step backward, he fell onto the bed and pulled Angela on top of him.

Grabbing her hips, he pulled her tight against him. "You make me nuts," he growled. "Your body is so pliant and willing. I've never met such incredibly inviting lips. You need me as much as I need you."

His words dissolved the last of Angela's reluctance. She gave in.

He kissed her neck and moved his mouth lower. Slipping his arms around her he rolled her beneath him. He unbuttoned her silk blouse and pulled her lace bra away from her flesh. "Your breasts are white as cream," he whispered in her ear as he tugged on her nipple making it taut. "And these—" he rubbed the bud between his thumb and forefinger "—like peaches." Then he took her nipple into his mouth. Teasing, pulling and stroking her with his tongue until she thought she would scream from the sweet torture, she felt him become more engorged.

She placed her fingertips on his back and pressed his flesh so hard, she was certain she'd left marks, like a brand on his skin.

Suddenly Rafe stopped his hand as it was about to slip beneath her panties and tore his mouth from her breast. He pushed himself to his elbows and stared down at her. She saw his eyes were filled with confusion.

"I'm sorry," he said raspily.

Angela didn't know whether to cry or hit him. "No problem," she said, sitting up. Suddenly, she felt like a fool and an idiot as she smoothed her hair. Obviously, she had gotten much more carried away than he. She was guilty of incredibly unprofessional behavior and she might have just blown the biggest deal of her year. But she didn't care. Even if he hated her for it, she wouldn't have missed this moment for the world. Oddly enough, just knowing that a man could respond to a woman like Rafe had to her renewed her hope that somewhere, sometime in her life, she just might find love after all. Even if it wasn't with Rafe Whitten.

Angela knew the most important thing for her to do at this moment was to save face. "No harm done," she answered with cool sobriety.

Raking his hair with his fingers, Rafe stared at her. What kind of woman was she to bring him to the brink of near-rape on their first…all right…their second meeting, and then turn off her body's responses like a spigot?

He'd been with enough women to know that she had truly been turned on by him. And yet now she was so aloof, so businesslike, he wondered if her head and body were attached.

Surely she'd felt the spirit of this room, sensed the sacredness of this moment. He'd wanted to tell her that he'd never made love in this room to anyone...not even...

How very odd. For a moment, he'd forgotten Cheryl's name.

Angela studied the etchings of confusion on his face.

Looming before him like a hellish banshee, Cheryl's face brought Rafe's thoughts into clarity. *I'm in over my head. Way over.*

Moving off to the side so that Angela could sit up to button her blouse, Rafe noticed that the soft lights in her eyes had turned to granite. Though one part of him wanted to see that kind of love again, the other part told him this was all definitely for the best. "I guess I got carried away. It was just seeing this room through your eyes made me a bit...nostalgic."

Nostalgic? He calls the kiss of the century, "nostalgic"? I'd like to see what happens when he gets turned on. "It happens," she said flippantly as she buttoned the last button and stuffed her blouse beneath the skirt's waistband.

"Not to me it sure as hell doesn't," Rafe replied, angrily bolting off the bed. He started pacing. And he knew why. His body was so pent-up he felt as if he could tear down the house and rebuild it in an hour. But what he really wanted was to make love to this luscious woman for the next three days, nonstop. Then he wanted her to go away...forever. Her intensity made him crazy.

"That's good to know," Angela said, slipping her feet into her taupe pumps. She flipped her silver-blond hair off her face, and looking up she drove a hard stare into him. "Just so you know, this kind of thing has never happened to me either. I wouldn't want you to get the impression I have to sleep my way to high commissions."

"I wasn't thinking...." Rafe tried to explain but Angela interrupted him.

"I've got a pretty good idea what you were thinking," she replied, struggling to cool her fury. "You're right, though, nostalgia had a lot to do with our...temporary loss of common sense." She walked to the door. "Now, if you wouldn't mind. I'd like to see the rest of the house and make my appraisal. Then, I'll be going."

Rafe felt as if he and his emotions had been slung around the room like a racquetball. How did she manage it? Looking so cool and put together as if nothing had happened. Just seeing the nearly imperceptible tremble of her bottom lip, like a child who's been hurt, made him want to take her in his arms and smother her with so many kisses she'd never feel pain again. He wanted her to feel joy for some reason, but he couldn't for the life of him understand why. Such ideas were not part of the framework of the post-Cheryl Rafe Whitten. He was wiser now, he thought, as his eyes travelled from the floor up the length of Angela's shapely legs, her rounded hips, small waist and perfectly formed high breasts to her angel's face. He'd never wanted a woman this much. And he'd never wanted to get rid of a woman as quickly.

"Fine. Great," he said brightly as he followed her out the door and down the hallway to the renovated master bath. He pointed out the antique porcelain basin and the antique footed tub. The room was still decorated in rose pink and spring green, though updated for his more modern tastes, just the way his grandmother would have wanted.

They went downstairs. Angela made the last of her notes, checked the plumbing, electrical wiring and septic tank system. She inspected the horse barn, paying as little attention as possible to the fantastically beautiful horses Rafe raised and sold. She didn't want him to think that she was sentimental about animals, although she was. She was determined to come across as the business professional she knew she was.

"Don't you need to see the rest of the ranch?" Rafe asked as they exited the barn.

"No." Angela was proud of herself when she showed Rafe the thick file of survey papers and the extensive legal description of the ranch that Matt had provided for her. "As you can see, I'm well prepared."

"I do. So, what's our next step?"

That's up to you. "Once I get the comparable sales figures together, I'll call you back with a sale price, one I feel is fair both to you and to the buyer and one that will get us a quick sale. However, this is your property. The final decision is all yours. Then, I'll need to meet with you again for you to sign the papers."

"Couldn't you just leave them with Matt and I could sign when I come to town next time?"

Then I wouldn't get to see you, be with you. Experience this incredible place again. "That will be fine."

"Good. That saves us both...er, some time," Rafe stumbled when the afternoon sun glinted off her heavenly hair.

Angela extended her hand. It was the professional thing to do. "Thank you so much for your business, Mr. Whitten. I think you'll find our team nothing short of excellent."

"I'm sure of it," Rafe said, shaking her hand.

Angela turned abruptly and walked back to her car.

Just the sight of her swaying hips and the ethereal halo around her head caused him to march back to the horse barn. He whistled for Rising Star and the stallion came out of the barn and galloped across the corral to where Rafe was climbing the fence.

Hearing the sound of her car engine and the tires as they crunched on the gravel drive, Rafe knew that in moments she'd be gone. If he handled everything perfectly, he could very well never have to see or speak to Angela Morton again. He could forget the taste of her breast in his mouth and the sweet pressure of her lips on his.

I can forget her...like hell I can.

Jumping onto Rising Star's bare back, Rafe rode through the open gate, slid off to close it behind him and, then, remounting, turned the stallion toward the low rolling pasture to the south. There was only one thing Rafe could do right now to get Angela Morton out of his mind...ride like the devil.

Five

Angela gently inserted her left foot, then her right, into a pair of two-hundred-dollar designer winter-white pumps. Standing up, then carefully scrutinizing her feet and legs in the mirror in the shoe salon, she finally turned to Julia for approval. "What do you think?"

"For two hundred bucks, sale or no sale, they should change your life," Julia shrugged her shoulders. "But you're not Cinderella and those shoes aren't gonna make your 'mystery man' call you."

"I wasn't thinking that at all," Angela lied unconvincingly.

"Yeah, sure," Ilsa said waiting for the salesman to fit her with a pair of less expensive dressy-casual black flats.

Angela frowned at the shoes, no longer thrilled with the pre-Christmas-sale hunting expedition. "It's just that I really didn't think he was serious when he said he'd use

Matt Leads as his go-between. I mean, I am his agent and we have things we should be discussing."

"Like what?" Julia asked in the professional, analytical tone of voice she normally saved for the office. "Have you found him a buyer in the week and a half since you listed the ranch?"

"Well, not exactly, but I have placed some great ads in very popular magazines."

Julia rolled her eyes. "I was meaning to talk to you about the fact that you've now completely lost your mind obsessing over this guy. You're making some very weird business decisions lately."

Ilsa, always the mediator between her two headstrong friends, placed her hand empathetically on Angela's forearm. "I know you must have had a good reason."

Glaring at Julia, Angela said, "At least somebody still has faith in me."

Julia didn't flinch as she waited for an answer. "Well?"

"Sometimes you're so uncreative, Julia. Just because I've had a few off months lately doesn't mean I don't know what I'm doing. I've always managed to make an enviable living in real estate. The commission for this property alone will make up for all my losses. Have you considered the fact that Rafe's ranch will sell at just under a million, given the acreage, the small lake and the buildings? Movie stars and rock stars, their producers, managers and agents are leaving smoggy LA in droves. Colorado is frightfully expensive and Montana is too cold for a lot of Californians who've grown accustomed to warmer climates. Given the fact that there's still no personal income tax in Texas, and the land taxes in Waller County are low, it all creates the kind of place any Californian would like. Look at the invasion of stars, directors and writers swarming all over the West Texas Hills. And all that land has to be developed. Rafe's place has utilities, roads, even a satellite dish. It's too perfect for the right kind of person.''

Pleasantly overwhelmed by Angela's savvy assessment of the situation, Julia said, ''I take it all back. You really will sell it, and soon, probably. I should think you'd want to drag it all out a bit. Then you'd have more excuses to connect with him.''

''No way. He needs the money now.''

Beaming, with glimmers of hero worship in her eyes, Ilsa replied, ''How sweet…and unselfish of you.''

''She's being flat smart, is what she's doing,'' Julia said.

''Thanks,'' Angela replied.

''Darned right. You're a smart cookie when you want to be. Like you said, you're through with men.''

I did? Oh, God, I did. Angela forced a smile. ''Rafe has made it quite clear he's not interested in me… romantically, I mean.''

''I'm so happy to hear you say that, Angela. I can tell you've really grown since that last jerk…I mean relationship,'' Ilsa stumbled over her thoughts as if she were wearing oversize clown shoes.

Julia's sigh was heavy with exasperation. ''What she means is that you get so caught up in your nostalgic, romantic notions sometimes, that you forget to look at reality. Granted I haven't met Rafe, but just the fact that he's this cowboy like your great-grandfather…''

''I haven't let sentimentalities influence my behavior in the least,'' Angela cut in defensively.

''That's real good. Just don't weaken.''

''Hey, I'm a big girl. I don't ever want to be with someone who doesn't want to be with me. My relationship with

Rafe is strictly business." Though Angela smiled confidently at her friends, she couldn't help thinking about Rafe's kiss at that moment. Never had she been so certain about a man in her life. She'd believed he'd been heaven-sent, but he obviously wasn't getting the message. Maybe their timing was off. Maybe she had been reading him incorrectly. The truth of the matter was that Julia's comment had disturbed her. Too often, Angela was guilty of becoming enthralled with the romance and not with the man. Otherwise, she'd never have been through some of the disastrously unlucky relationships of the past.

"From now on, I'm going to be much more practical about my personal life. Romance is for other people who haven't learned their lesson yet," Angela said confidently.

"Atta girl," Julia patted her on the back.

Just then the shoe salesman who had reboxed a half dozen pairs of shoes interrupted their conversation. "And which pairs would you like today?"

Angela looked at Julia who nodded at Ilsa. In unison, they replied, "All of them."

Turning the corner off Post Oak Lane, Angela hit her garage door opener and parked the car. As she entered the house through the kitchen door, she deposited her car keys in an old sterling silver butler's tray. Then she heard a thunderous pounding down the staircase.

"Rebel!" she yelled.

The dog came galloping at her and with his usual greeting practically knocked her down while she petted him. She ruffled his ears fondly. "Are you ready for your walk? Ready to get the mail?"

Rebel reared up on his hind legs and standing nearly as tall as she, put his front paws on her shoulders and licked her face. "Nice kisses, Rebel."

Angela went to the broom closet, took out Rebel's leash and grabbed the front-door keys. Rebel was so excited to leave, she knew he couldn't wait a moment longer.

Just as she reached the door, the phone rang. She halted momentarily, but Rebel was panting heavily and tugging on the leash. "I'll get it later, Rebel. The machine will pick up."

Opening the door for Rebel, who happily bounded out the front brick walkway, Angela didn't give the phone call a second thought.

Hanging up the phone with a rush of hostile breath directed mostly toward himself for succumbing to a momentary weakness, Rafe immediately dialed a second number. As he listened to the phone ringing on the opposite end, he sorted through an ever growing stack of bills. There was only one envelope that did not herald a threatening warning of "Urgent"; a Christmas card from Matt Leads. Rafe tore open the envelope just as he heard a woman's voice say, "Matthew Leads's office."

"Hey, Jennie. Is Matt in?"

"Hello, Mr. Whitten. Uh, he's in a meeting," Jennie, the efficient, soft-spoken secretary hedged.

Rafe knew instantly Matt was no doubt flailing his arms at Jennie warning her not to put Rafe's call through. "Jennie, if you keep lying for him, you'll go to hell."

After a long pause, Matt came on the line. "I'm not taking your calls, Rafe. If you want to know what's happening with your property sale, call your agent yourself."

"You're the one who put me in this spot, Matt. You sent her out here without consulting me."

"You could have signed with someone else, but you're too mule-headed to admit you've got that girl under your skin. Too bad she doesn't know it."

"What do you mean?"

"Maybe if you slept with her and quit fantasizing about her, you'd find out she's just like any other girl. Then you could get on with your business."

"Do you honestly think that's all there is? Lust?"

"Don't knock lust. Lust has value," Matt smirked to himself. "Even if it's more than that, you'll know for sure and you'll still be able to get focused."

"I'm selling Rising Star," Rafe said, his voice raspy with emotion. "I got an offer from a breeder in Kentucky who knew about his sire's, Rising Sun's, racing record. Having a Derby winner in his ancestry could get me nearly fifty grand."

"Good God, man. I know things are tough, but well, couldn't you sell off one of the others? You and Rising Star are so close."

"I haven't found any takers. Maybe it's because the holidays are coming up."

"Good point. That money would see you through the next six months. Even give you a chance to keep the company's skeleton crew together. What was the last word from the telephone company?"

"They're willing to meet with me right after the first of the year. They've signed a non-disclosure agreement and I sent them a fax with explicit details about the embezzlement and what I still owe my original investors. These days I don't feel comfortable without plans B, C, D and E already working."

Matt paused for a long moment. "I know this has been rough on you. Why don't you give yourself a break and call Angela?"

"She wasn't home," Rafe answered in a low voice.

"Try her again," Matt encouraged.

"Maybe. Thanks for listening, Matt. Guess I just needed a sounding board."

"We all do from time to time. Well, I've gotta go. My desk is piled so high with work, it looks like a mountain range," Matt said, chuckling, and hung up.

Glancing at Angela's phone number on the business card she'd left with him gave Rafe another idea. He pulled out the white pages, looked up A. Morton and found her address on Post Oak Lane. He dialed her number again. This time Angela answered.

"Hello."

Rafe opened his mouth to speak, but just hearing her voice unsettled him so thoroughly, his voice croaked as if he were being strangled.

Taken aback by the odd-sounding voice on the other end of the line, Angela frowned and then blared back into the receiver, "Pervert!" Then she slammed the phone down.

Rebel sensed Angela's fear and instantly stood protectively beside her. She patted his head and bent down to give him a bear hug around his neck. "It's all right, fella. Just another phone creep."

Then she walked to the front door and armed the security system. "Just the same, there's nothing wrong with being extra careful."

Angela climbed the stairs carrying the shoes she'd bought. She should have been thrilled about the bargains she'd found today. She should be excited about getting out her Christmas decorations, sorting through everything and deciding where she'd put the tree this year. Instead, all she thought about was that phone call. It didn't bother her that some preteen boy was making prank calls. She wasn't frightened or worried that it was anything else but that. What upset her most was the fact that when the phone rang it wasn't Rafe Whitten.

How long was it going to take for her to get this man she barely knew out of her mind? How thick was her skull that she couldn't understand he was not interested in her? And why on earth was it that even the thought of his smile, the remembered scent of his musky skin made her anxious, tense and feeling as if she would explode if she didn't hear from him, see him soon?

There was nothing else to do, she thought as Rebel came bounding up the stairs behind her.

"I need a very cold shower."

Six

Dialing Angela's number from his cellular phone, Rafe heard the phone being picked up by the recorder. "Angela, this is Rafe. I know you're home, so why aren't you picking up this call. Angela? Are you there?"

Dripping wet and with shampoo suds flowing down her bare back, Angela picked up the extension next to her bed. "Rafe? I was in the shower and it took me a few moments to get to the phone," she explained wrapping a towel around her body. She shivered in the chilly room. The temperature must have dropped considerably since sundown, she thought. Tonight would be a good night for a fire.

"In the shower? I've heard that before," he answered a bit caustically. "Are you sure you aren't avoiding my calls?"

"How could I? You haven't called."

What is there about this woman that makes me lose all my common sense? "It was a joke," he covered himself.

"Oh."

"I'd like to see you tonight. That is if you don't have other plans," he said tentatively. *If she was in the shower, maybe she has a date.* "Carrabas isn't too far from here," he turned around and looked toward Post Oak Lane.

From here? "Rafe, where are you calling me from?"

"Your front door."

Angela swallowed hard. "You're downstairs?" She quickly rolled the miniblinds open and looked out. She saw his truck and then a man's shadow cast from the automatic porch lights. "You're downstairs!"

"I said that, yes," he chuckled. "I tried to call earlier, but you weren't home."

Suddenly she remembered the call just before she walked Rebel. "You could have left a message. I could have called you back."

"You could come downstairs and let me in. I didn't wear a jacket and it's getting colder by the second out here. Would you mind?"

Flustered over his sudden presence when she'd been wishing for exactly this to happen, she hung up the phone. "No, I don't mind." Then she realized he hadn't heard a word she'd said. She picked up the phone. "I'm on my way down." She hung up again.

Quickly, she grabbed a second towel and wrapped it turban style around her cold, wet and soapy hair as she raced down the staircase to the door.

She unlocked the door and instantly set off the alarm. "Oh dear!" She shut the door, leaving Rafe still standing on the front step holding a bottle of chardonnay. She disarmed the security system, opened the door, grabbed his sleeve and nearly yanked him indoors.

"It's freezing out there!" she exclaimed.

Rafe smiled broadly at her. "You really were in the shower!" He began chuckling. Then he laughed out loud at her.

"What's so funny?" she demanded.

"Who socked you?" he howled. When she continued to stare at him dumbly, he said, "You have mascara smeared under your eyes."

"Oh, that's no big deal," she replied wiping her fingers under the bottom row of lashes.

He put his hands on her shoulders and scooted her over to the antique mirrored hall tree in the foyer. "It's going to take more than that."

Staring at the reflection of a woman who looked as if she'd rubbed nearly her entire face and half her forehead with burned cork, Angela threw her hands to her face. "I'll be right back!" she gasped and lunged toward the staircase.

Rafe couldn't help laughing as the towel over her hair untwisted and the towel around her body began slipping over her breasts. Angela fumbled with one and then the other in her struggle to hide her embarrassment.

"This is all your fault, Rafe Whitten. If you'd had any manners at all, you'd have let me know you were coming and I wouldn't look like this."

"You're absolutely right, Angela, and I take total blame for every bit of it," he yelled up the stairs as she reached the second-story landing. From his vantage point he could see up her bare legs to the fleshy part of her buttocks and as she scrambled for control of the towel on her head, he saw her left breast slip out from under the terry-cloth. Though the sight of her voluptuous body only made his need for her surge, she also looked like a little girl blushing with anger and frustration. Without her knowing it, she'd just endeared herself to him in a way he hadn't thought possible.

This is a terrible turn of events, he thought, as he found his way into the kitchen, opened one drawer after another until he found a corkscrew and opened the bottle of wine. He poured two glasses. "I was supposed to seduce you, Angela, and get you out of my system forever."

He walked into the living room and stopped short. He'd expected to see a very feminine apartment, with stacks of frilly pillows, lace curtains and dried roses that had long lost their scent or value as far as he was concerned. Instead, he found the kind of western mountain-looking home he wanted to make for himself someday, once he was back on his feet again—maybe somewhere in the hill country or even the Rockies—but his dream was so far from the reality of his life right now, he didn't dare think that far ahead.

Noticing a stack of wood in the log carrier, Rafe set himself to making a fire in the fireplace to take the chill out of the room. As the flames licked the nubby oak bark, Rafe sat back on his heels pensively sipping his wine. He didn't hear Angela as she padded into the room in sock-covered feet.

"Make yourself at home, Rafe," she said curtly.

He chuckled to himself and then rose carrying a glass of wine to her. "Don't be angry. You don't wear it well."

"What's that supposed to mean?" she asked snatching the glass of wine and then walking around him to sit by the fire where the heat would finish drying her hair.

Rafe's eyes followed her. Without makeup, her moon-beam-colored hair backlit by the tangerine flames, and dressed in a tunic-styled angora sweater and matching leggings of the palest peach, she looked like the kind of pixie who haunted the earth at twilight time. Or at least that was the story he remembered from his childhood. "Some women only look good when they're angry, which isn't good. You look best with a smile."

"Thank you," she replied, taking a sip of wine. *I think.* "Now, why are you here?"

"I wanted to talk to you about my ranch."

"You couldn't do this during business hours? You couldn't have had your CPA fax me your inquiries? You had to come all the way into town, at night, wine in hand, to talk about business? I don't think so, Rafe." She blasted him with a disturbingly probing look.

Suddenly feeling unsure of the wisdom of being in the same room with her, Rafe began to feel his attraction to Angela getting out of control. Maybe he should have stayed away after all, he thought, as his hands ached to sink into her silky hair.

As she traced her forefinger around the rim of the wine glass and then licked off the excess, Rafe could almost taste her sweet lips. Damnation! But he'd never experienced anything like this forceful urge to take her in his arms and kiss her. After ten days of staying away from her, he thought he'd proved that she couldn't possibly have this much power over him. And how did she do it? What was her trick? There had to be an answer to this mystery and he was determined to reveal the logic behind it all.

"I feel that you and I have gotten off on the wrong foot about everything. We're both adults and I thought that perhaps if I apologized for my behavior—"

He wants to take back the kiss of the century? "You have nothing to apologize for. We didn't start out doing business, if you remember..."

"Oh, I remember," he smiled sensuously at her. "But after that, I mean. At my house. I was out of line. I just don't want you to think badly of me.'' *If you think of me at all.*

Sighing heavily, Angela was conscious of her bare breasts under the thin angora. The sensation of the soft wool against her skin was tantalizing. She could feel her nipples hardening, but she knew the reaction had little to do with the sweater. Rafe's blue-green eyes had turned that smoky color that told her he was thinking about kissing her. Right now, that's all she wanted from him. Just one more kiss…then another…and another.

Angela, seize control of your emotions! This man doesn't care about you the way you want. Tell him to leave. Tell him he's your client and be done with it.

''I could never think badly of you, Rafe,'' she found herself saying. ''In fact, I think you're quite noble. Selling your home is never easy. The memories attached to every cubic inch of that ranch house will always remain with you. But sadly, nothing will ever take the place of that particular house. Believe me.''

''You sound as if you know firsthand what I'm going through.''

''I do,'' she said and went on to explain how difficult it had been when she'd been faced with the same problem.

Awestruck by her story, Rafe moved over to sit on the floor next to her, Indian-style. Their knees touched. ''You were only eighteen. I don't know how you had the strength. That took incredible courage, Angela,'' he said reaching out to touch her leg.

Not once did she feel the sexual impulse she thought he'd radiate with his touch. Instead, she sensed heartfelt empathy; a connection of two kindred spirits who'd been forced by fate to endure the same pain.

''I did what I had to do at the time to survive. And I did. I managed to keep all my family's things, however.

I guess that was why I was saddened that you'd been selling your antiques. Such things are treasures to people like us, not just possessions or pieces of furniture. I know this will sound really odd to you, but I believe that our surroundings, houses, cars, furniture absorb some of our energies, our personality as we live with them for long periods of time. I'm not a throwaway junkie like a lot of people today. I don't believe in discarding bits of myself."

"I've...never heard anyone talk quite like you, Angela. You really are a different kind of woman. I think much the same way, though when my back's been up against a wall, I'll do anything to survive. You've been luckier than I."

"Maybe." *Only time will tell.*

Her brown eyes were limpid pools on the verge of tears, but he didn't know why. Intuition told him he'd stirred her feelings for him. He wanted to believe her emotions were genuine and that she had no ulterior motives. He'd been played for a fool before; he'd fallen for even more stunning beauty, more theatrical displays of what he'd thought were heart songs only to discover every word spoken to him had been false.

Still he felt himself drawing nearer to Angela, wanting to taste every inch of her body. Believing that once he made love to her, he would understand her true motivations where he was concerned. Her kisses had been more than wanton desire. She'd touched his heart in a way he'd never believed possible. Maybe that was the magic about her that had drawn him back to Angela Morton when he'd thought he knew better than to be within ten miles of her. Yet here he was, sitting face-to-face with her, their legs touching, their eyes searching for answers neither was ready to give at this point.

Questioning again Matt's wisdom that if he made love to Angela he would discover she was no different than any other woman, Rafe found himself moving his mouth closer to hers.

Angela felt her icy resolve melt instantaneously with Rafe's sensual downward glance at her lips. She watched as he struggled to look in her eyes, but he found the intensity of their gaze as impossible to bear as she did. Moving her mouth closer to his, she watched his eyes roll back in his head and his long-lashed eyelids descend as he gave himself over totally to her.

The kiss was more than compelling, it was indulgent and completely satiating. Slanting his mouth over hers, he took her lips between his, softly nibbling her bottom lip, forcing shock waves of torrid desire streaking straight to her loins. Prodding her mouth open with his tongue to allow himself entry to her, commandingly he took her tongue like a warrior bent on victory.

His arms clamped around her back and he pulled her to his chest. Rather than holding her in a vise, she sensed an imperceptible ambiguity that made her think he didn't really want her after all.

Feeling that bliss was kissing Rafe and nothing less and that she could never let him go, Angela uttered the most courageous words of her life, "I think you should go, Rafe."

Caught in an eerie half-world between dream and reality, Rafe barely heard what she'd said. Instead, he plunged his tongue into her honey-sweet mouth once again. No matter how he tried to deny it, every one of Angela's kisses was like the first kiss.

Angela broke away. She forced herself to say the blasphemous words, "I really mean it, Rafe. I want you to leave."

Seven

"Harpies from hell couldn't make me leave you now. But I'm not going to force myself on you, Angela. I thought you wanted me as much as I want you." Delving to the core of her heart, his blue-green eyes plumbed her psyche, stripping it of all defenses, all resolve. "Tell me what you really want, Angela."

"I want…" Her voice faltered, knowing she couldn't lie to him. Not to Rafe. Not when there was a chance they could make the magic of love endure for more than just a night. She sensed he didn't believe it, but she did.

Her eyes filled with tears. She was afraid to push him away when they might have just now found each other. She remembered what her parents had taught her; that to take risks was all life was about. She put her reputation on the line hundreds of time at work and made impossible deals happen. She'd risked her feelings before, but not like this. With Rafe it was different. This time her heart was on the line.

She closed her eyes forcing her tears to ebb.

"That's what I thought," Rafe said gruffly and before she knew what was happening, he'd slid one strong arm around her shoulders and the other under her legs. He lifted her like a weightless rag doll. Turning away from the fire, he walked out of the room and started up the stairs.

"What…are you doing?" she stammered.

"What I should have done the first night we met." Then he possessively took her lips between his and kissed her with an urgent passion she'd never experienced before.

She kissed him back with equal fervor, not wanting even to breathe again without his lips next to hers. Abandoning all her brave resolutions, she suddenly couldn't wait to feel him lie next to her.

"You see, Angela, you do want me even more than you're willing to admit to yourself. There's nothing I wouldn't do for you right now and nothing you wouldn't do for me. I want to know and explore every inch of your body, inside and out. I want to know what turns you on and what you want from me to bring you to ecstasy. I want what we share to be more moving than anything you've ever experienced with any other man."

Without waiting for an answer, he took her mouth rapaciously, demanding that her body tell him what he wanted to know. Her hands had encircled his neck and now their muscles tensed, as she pulled herself into him forcing his tongue even deeper into her mouth.

She could feel Rafe's heart pounding at breakneck speed when they reached the bedroom door. "I'm not stepping foot into this room until you tell me you want me, Angela," he demanded.

"I want...you," she whispered.

His eyes were glazed with desire as they scoured her face. "Louder. I never want you to think back on this night with anything less than the clearest head."

"I want you, Rafe. More than you could ever imagine," she replied looking deeply into his eyes.

Carrying her to the bed, he gently placed her on the white blanket cover. Golden light puddled from a small antique cut-crystal lamp on the dark mahogany nightstand.

Watching the night shadows play along the planes of his face, Angela held her breath as he kicked off his boots, peeled off his socks and unzipped his jeans. He was wearing no underwear, and she was surprised to find him fully aroused. She closed her eyes.

"No, Angela. I want you to look at me," he said slowly unbuttoning his shirt. "See how much I want you," he ordered huskily as he moved over her.

She felt his hands slip inside her leggings and grab the soft sides of her hips before peeling the spandex cotton from her legs. Then he purposefully moved his hips next to her naked thigh so that she could feel the length and fullness of him. He nuzzled her neck and placed tiny hot, wet kisses around her like a rope of pearls. In one motion he yanked the angora sweater over her head and tossed it carelessly to the side of the bed.

Her skin flushed with desire and need from head to toe. Angela could nearly feel beads of perspiration between her shoulder blades and breasts. Already she was pulsing with anticipation. If she lived to be a hundred, she knew she would never want a man as much as she desperately wanted Rafe Whitten tonight.

The engulfing power of her desire frightened her enough to ask, "Shouldn't we turn out the light?"

His blue eyes bored into hers. "I want to look at you, Angela, and I want you to look at me. When I finally take you, I want you to look in my eyes and know that I'm making you mine."

His sensual words nearly drove her over the edge. Mercifully, he lowered his gaze to her lips just then and rapaciously captured her mouth. The feverish duel he'd performed with her tongue began again and this time she held nothing back. She let him slide his tongue up and down as he drank her juices. Then without warning, the kiss ended as he left her but only to blaze his searing tongue against the alabaster skin along the column of her throat. Then further down over her chest until he found her nipples.

Simultaneously, his hand cupped her breast and kneaded it. Searing blasts of carnal cravings erupted deep in her loins. A moist dew slipped out of her, wetting her swollen bud in anticipation of his entry. She felt her legs automatically open for him. Angela was beyond reason. She was consumed with sexual fervor.

Feeling Rafe's lips and tongue prod then nip every inch of her round breasts, caused her to press his head into her all the more. She ached for him.

She put her hands on his hips urging him to enter her, but Rafe resisted.

"Not yet."

His head went between her legs teasing, licking, stroking and nibbling her into such insanely wondrous pleasure, Angela thought she'd never recover from the rapture.

This can't end, ever. It just can't, she thought as she sank her fingertips into his thick hair. She didn't dare press him any deeper into her and yet she couldn't help herself. Gyrating her hips she held her breath as she felt the first wave of pleasure spread over her like a gentle breeze, then it suddenly turned into a ferociously powerful tornado of sensations.

Spiraling higher as if she were leaving her body, Angela allowed herself to flow with this storm called Rafe. She twisted beneath him as he expertly intensified her pleasure a second time. This time she plunged downward as if she were being sucked into a whirlpool. Suddenly she was back in her body.

"Open your eyes and look at me, Angela." His voice was velvety yet husky with sexuality as he moved over her. "Let me know I have everything you have to give."

Feeling his hand searching for her entrance, then his finger sink into her, Angela's eyes flew open.

Startled to find his eyes brimming with love and gentle tears at the corners, she instinctively closed her eyes, blinded by the brightness of the miracle she was witnessing.

No one loves that much. Not even I.

"Open your eyes, Angela," he commanded.

When she did as he asked, her heart felt his every thought like tiny shock waves bent upon opening the iron gates she'd erected when her parents had died. Not until this moment had she realized how much she'd closed herself off completely from love. Subconsciously she'd always picked the wrong kind of man because her heart hadn't been ready for the real thing. Rafe was showing her she'd never been in love before.

As he at last sank inside her, Angela burst into tears of joy. It was as if she could feel his feelings, understand his wants and desires and blend her mind with his enough to even dream his dreams. She and Rafe had become one.

It was the most moving and deeply touching event of her life.

Thrusting against her warm, moist walls, Rafe couldn't look away from Angela's eyes. He placed his hands on either side of her face, propping himself on his elbows and with his thumbs he wiped away each of her tears as they slipped out the corners. His gesture was so tender, so heartfelt, she couldn't stop the easy smile that crept to her lips.

"I..." she started to say as her heart opened wider to him.

"Shh." He placed his forefinger on her lips. "Don't say anything. Your eyes tell me all I need to know."

At that moment, his stroking became incredibly intense. He lowered his head and sucked her nipple once again. He slid his hand down and spread her wings apart and simultaneously rubbed her bud and pushed himself even deeper inside. Angela thought she'd go out of her mind with the pleasure he was giving her.

Rafe's eyelids slowly sank as he pushed himself as far into Angela as their bodies would allow. Sweat bloomed over the length of him as he shivered with the onslaught of his climax. "Angel..." he moaned her name as his back arched like a cat and his pelvis drove into her.

Her heart at ramming speed, muscles tautly strung, Angela's panting suddenly stopped. Rolling through her like an underwater riptide she finally exploded. Like a tsunami he engulfed her from above and beneath. She pressed her hands against the corded muscles of his back and pulled him down gently on her. The sheer weight of him pressing against her was more delicious than his kiss or the sex because for the first time, she felt she possessed him.

Their skin glistening with sweat and sweet juices, Angela kept her arms around Rafe as he rolled exhausted onto his side. She smoothed his tousled dark hair from his face thinking that at this moment he looked like an angel himself.

Raphael. Highest of the archangels. Reigning above Michael and Gabriel, Raphael was the responsible one, the angel with the strongest shoulders and the deepest commitment.

From this day forward, that was how Angela wanted to think of Rafe. Though he'd called her "angel," she knew now he was more deserving of that name.

Angela had never been made love to like this. She'd never known two bodies could create such a sexual, almost spiritual, awakening. She wondered if it was possible to recreate this feeling again. She hoped so. She wanted to know that this miraculous connection between herself and Rafe was sacred. Certainly their meeting that night on her birthday was fated to happen. Not for a minute would she ever give credence to the idea that they'd simply stumbled onto each other.

It was all too wondrous. Too incredible. Angela smiled as she thought about how much she'd already come to love this man she barely knew.

Rafe opened his eyes to see Angela smiling at him. Her eyes were filled with so much love and willingness to give her heart to him, it frightened him.

What's happened to me? To my plan? It wasn't supposed to turn out like this. I was supposed to discover she's just like every other girl I've known. I've never seen anyone look at me like this before...as if she'd give me not just her heart, but her soul, too. Why does she look at me as if she could make love to me all night long...all life long?

"Is something wrong?" Rafe asked tentatively, still not understanding Angela's thoughts.

"No. Nothing," she answered sweetly while playing with a lock of his hair.

He reached up and touched her bottom lip. "My kisses bruised you. I'm sorry." Placing his hand on her nape he pulled her down to him and kissed her deeply.

Brushing his chest with her breasts, Angela crawled over him and kissed him back. Slowly, she lowered herself onto him as her tongue sought the interior of his mouth. In moments the temperature of her skin rose a degree, then another. Angela knew exactly what she wanted. She slid her face to the crook of his neck and kissed him in that shallow well where his pulse was dangerously close to the surface. In this vulnerable valley she could measure his heart's response to her touch.

His breath caught in his throat as she reached lower and encircled him with her fingers. Massaging him, caressing him, she brought him to life again. With painstaking deliberateness, Angela pressed light kisses on his chest, rib cage, stomach, abdomen and then lower where she found him swollen with desire.

"Now it's my turn to send you back to heaven, Raphael," she said as she covered him with her mouth.

Eight

Awaking halfway between heaven and earth, Angela was surprised the next morning to find herself lying in Rafe's arms. Though she'd only felt it for a millisecond at one point while they were making love, she'd sensed the enormity of their experience had frightened him somehow.

Too many times, she'd seen panic in a man's eyes, just when he was about to bolt and run. Fear of real intimacy was something she'd witnessed in her own reflection more than once. She knew she was right. She hoped she was wrong.

Just then Rafe opened his eyes. "Mornin', sunshine," he yawned and pulled her head into the crook of his arm. He kissed the top of her head. "I hadn't intended to fall asleep. I think you wore me out," he chuckled and rubbed his sleepy eyes.

I was right! He did want to leave. "You don't make a practice of sleeping over?" She wanted to feel as casual about their affair as he sounded, but she didn't. Something awesome had happened to her last night. Her intuition told her that something monumental and life-changing had occurred. She was disappointed he didn't feel it, too.

"It's been a long time since I..." he began as a flash of Cheryl's deceitful face broke off his thoughts. He detested being haunted by a woman whose character was nowhere near Angela's class, but the Cheryl "wringer" taught him never to move too quickly again. He'd thought he was head over heels with Cheryl. In the end, she'd choreographed the entire relationship. How could he be sure Angela wasn't doing the same?

Besides, I hadn't planned for last night to work out this way. I was supposed to get you out of my system.

"'...been a long time since' who, Rafe?" she asked wondering what had happened to end his last relationship.

"I sleep alone," he replied in clipped, hollow tones.

"Me, too," she said.

Angela's answer unexpectedly gave Rafe a sense of elation. Refusing to allow Cheryl's memory to control another second of his life, Rafe playfully pulled Angela onto his chest. "Come here, you vixen," he chuckled, grabbed her hips and settled her squarely in the center of his pelvis. He grinned mischievously. "Well, don't look now, but there's a man in your bed. So much for sleeping alone, huh?"

But do you love me? You never came close to saying the words, Rafe.

A smile struggled onto her lips. "I'd like to indulge you," she paused. *In fact, I can barely hold myself back.* "But I have a nine o'clock appointment this morning." She kissed his cheek quickly and scrambled out of his arms.

The top sheet was twisted around her leg and his thigh

in such a way that wherever she moved, he went with her. Kicking the sheet only made it worse. Angela tried to roll out of the mess, but ended up more tied to Rafe than when she started.

"I don't believe this," she sighed, frustrated.

"Face it, you're bound to me forever," he laughed.

Jerking her head around to face him, she said, "I'll get out of it, trust me." Then she went back to the business of escape.

Rafe felt as if she'd thrown ice water on his face. Obviously, his plan had backfired more than he'd thought. He was obsessed with Angela, but she'd worked *him* out of *her* system. She acted as if she couldn't wait to get away from him.

"Stop!" he demanded. "Here, let me do it." He bent around her, lifting the sheet out from under his hips then untwisted the material from her leg. "There. You're free now."

Angela stood quickly and went to the antique rocker in the corner and yanked the long cotton T-shirt off the seat where she'd laid it several days ago. Pulling the shirt over her head, she asked, "Would you like coffee for breakfast? What do you normally have?"

"Three eggs, sausage, flapjacks, coffee, juice…biscuits and gravy if you have them. The usual."

Angela's head popped out the neck of the T-shirt. Her eyes were as big as saucers. "That's the usual? What do you eat when you're really hungry?"

Rafe crossed his arms behind his head and let his eyes travel lustfully over every inch of her exposed body.

Angela yanked the long T-shirt down over her waist, then her hips, until the bottom edge covered the very tops of her thighs.

"What's the matter? It's not like I didn't see or taste every inch of you last night."

That was then. This is now. "I told you. I have to get going. And if I remember correctly, you have just a few animals to feed."

He smiled and threw the sheet back revealing everything Angela didn't want to see right now. He strutted over to her, reveling in her discomfort. He put his arms around her and pulled her into him. "They're just fine. What I want to make sure is that you're all right."

"Why wouldn't I be?"

He put his finger under her chin and lifted her face to his. "Don't play games with me, Angela. You're upset about something. If I did anything to displease you tell me know. I want us to be open and straightforward with each other. Tell me why you want me to leave."

"Well, I don't exactly want you to leave." *I want you to tell me that I'm special. That what we shared was important to you. I want to be able to tell you how much I'm already in love with you. But that's not how people play this game. It's too soon to say these things. I don't want you to run away from me before we get started.* "It's just that I really do have to get ready for this meeting."

"And you swear that's all it is?"

"Yes." *For now.*

"Then you'll have dinner with me Friday night?"

But Friday is two days away. What's wrong with tomorrow night? Or the next night? I want to see you tonight. "Friday sounds just great."

"Friday it is then," he kissed her tenderly reminding her of the tingling sensation his lips created. "I won't keep you any longer." He went to the bedside, picked up his jeans and pulled them on. Sticking his arms through his sleeves and putting on his socks and boots, he was ready to leave in less than three minutes.

He motioned toward the door with his head. "I'll just be goin' then, ma'am," he drawled and grinned wickedly at her. "I'll be by myself if you think you might want to call while I'm driving off into the sunrise."

Angela couldn't help laughing as he crossed to the door and opened it. "Where will we go Friday?"

"I'll surprise you," he winked.

"What I meant was what should I wear?"

"Me." He blew her a kiss and with one last look, he was gone.

Never had Angela been filled with so much confusion. His last gaze was filled with sensual longing. But where was the love she'd seen last night?

Two days was an incredibly long time for her to wait to find it again.

Wearing a dressy but casual black silk jacket, black silk slacks and black heels, Angela paced the gray-and-turquoise Indian rug she'd bought at a Hopi Indian reservation near the Grand Canyon last year. Rafe had left a message with the receptionist that morning, while she was on the phone with a client, that he'd pick her up at seven-thirty for dinner.

It was now eight-fifteen and Rafe had not shown up. She didn't know if she should be worried or angry. He'd given the receptionist his cellular phone number, but after dialing it four times she was still getting the same recording stating that he was "out of reach" at the moment. There was no answer at the house either.

Angela had been stood up before. Being part of the singles' world demanded that one must experience such things at least once. However, she'd wanted to believe

Rafe was too considerate and too much of a gentleman to display such bad manners. Since their first meeting, she'd sensed a deeply felt integrity in him. Or at least she'd wanted to think that highly of him.

Perhaps Julia and Ilsa were right. Too many times Angela had been guilty of projecting her own good qualities onto undeserving men. Was she fashioning her own illusion of what she wanted Rafe to be? She'd certainly done it before. Was he trying to break away from her that next morning like she'd sensed? Or was she the guilty party?

"It's a wonder anyone ever has a relationship at all. These things are so...tough!"

Feeling her forehead break out in nervous perspiration, Angela went to the kitchen and poured herself a small glass of white wine. Putting the cork in the bottle, she only now remembered this was one of the bottles from Rafe's wine cellar. She'd barely tasted the buttery smooth wine then, because she'd been so intent on Rafe. For the life of her she couldn't remember much of what was said...only what was *not* said.

It wasn't that Angela was used to having men tell her they loved her, either before, during or after sex. She wasn't so weak that she was looking for approval, but with Rafe, it was different. Everything was different.

Rafe had touched a place inside her she hadn't known existed and it was driving her crazy wondering if she'd had the same effect on him.

Granted, she hadn't actually told *him* that she loved *him.* She'd always thought it best that the man say something first. Even she was guilty of never trusting stories from her girlfriends when they'd explained they were the one to say something first. There was always the chance the guy *didn't* feel the same way and only responded that he did to keep peace or get more sex.

Angela knew all these things, yet she'd almost blown it.

But he *stopped* me.

For a brief moment that night, Angela had seen what being loved by Rafe could be like. His blue eyes had looked as open, vulnerable and loving as a tiny infant's. Yet, when he placed his finger on her lips, he was telling her something.

But what? That it was too soon? That he wanted to be the one to declare his love to her? That this "thing" they had was not love, just sex? Did he want her, or not? Did he care for her, or not?

For two days these questions had plagued Angela. She thought she was going out of her mind.

Suddenly, the sky lit up as a bolt of lightning streaked across the night sky. Wrapping her arms around herself, Angela couldn't help thinking that all of this added up to loudly pealing warning bells in her mind. She remembered too well that horrid tragic night her parents had died.

Angela had been waiting and pacing then, just as she was now. She waited through the lightning storm until nearly dawn, sensing all the while that something was not right. Her parents should have landed in Ruidosa by nine. She called the airport and found that half the lines in New Mexico were down due to lightning and high winds. As the night progressed the same storm moved over Texas and cut off the electricity in a third of San Antonio. Fearful of the worst, Angela became frantic. Near dawn her fears were confirmed. Her parents had crashed. No one on board the small private plane had survived.

Angela looked at her watch and discovered it was twenty to nine. Thunder rumbled through the house, rattling the windowpanes. Angela jumped as another streak of lightning split the sky. Terrified that she was reliving her own past, she grabbed her raincoat, purse and car keys. She didn't care if Rafe didn't have one iota of the intense caring she had for him, she was determined to search all night if she had to. When she found Rafe, she would demand the truth.

"And the best place to start is at his own ranch."

None of the lights were on in the ranch house when Angela drove up and parked the car. The pelting rain had not started until she was north of Cypress, Texas. Now her windshield wipers barely kept pace.

The rain blurred all images as Angela drove slowly toward what she thought was a light in the horse barn. None of the outdoor halogen lights were on to illuminate the drive, corral or large barn. She realized the electricity was off.

Driving the car as close to the corral as she could, Angela turned off the engine and got out. She ran through the wind and rain to the entrance of the horse barn.

Two green lanterns cast minimal light across Rafe's back as he leaned over the white mare who was lying on a fresh mound of hay.

Watching Rafe gently administer medicine to the mare calmed Angela's own worries. Quietly she entered the barn not wanting to disturb, but mesmerized by the cooing sounds Rafe was making.

Whispering softly to the horse and without ceasing his long stroking caresses, Rafe tenderly eased the horse's fears. "It'll be just fine, Heartsong. Drink up."

He used a turkey baster to inject a full plunger of medicine down the mare's throat. "I made this especially for you. My granddaddy made the same concoction for me when I felt like you do."

The horse whinnied.

"I know, it tastes like rotted roots, which is practically what's in it, but it works. We'll beat this nasty fever...you and I together. I promise."

"Is she going to be all right?" Angela finally asked, her concern for Heartsong growing each time the mare moaned.

Startled, Rafe spun around. "What the blazes are you doing there?"

"I...thought we had a date."

"A date?" He spat the question out angrily. "When my mare is on the verge of pneumonia?"

"I waited..." *You have no idea how terrifying storms are for me. My pain was just as excruciating as yours is for you. I was afraid you were dead.* "I didn't know about Heartsong, Rafe. When you didn't answer your phone I thought..." *God! I thought some awful things.*

His face contorted with worry and fear, he suddenly realized what she was saying. "I'd forgotten about the date. I was so worried about Heartsong. The vet was here late last night and early this morning. She's already had two large injections of antibiotics. If she doesn't break the fever tonight..." His voice was filled with sadness. "I'm afraid there won't be much hope."

Angela stood over Rafe and Heartsong, then dropped to her knees. She put her hand on Rafe's shoulder. "Don't let yourself even think that way. She's going to be fine."

Rafe was so intensely involved with ministering to the mare, he hadn't heard a word Angela had said.

His eyes red from strain and tears and wearing a thick growth of stubble, he looked beaten and weary as if he hadn't slept in nights. She felt utterly helpless to comfort him. "What can I do to help?"

"Go away."

"What?"

Turning toward her, his eyes were flinty. "Can't you see you'll just be in the way? What do you know about horses? You haven't been where I've been. Over the years I've done everything I could to save my horses, but they get sick sometimes. Especially the mares." Looking down at Heartsong, his voice deepened with sorrow. "I lost my first mare when she was giving birth to a stillborn foal. I was twelve. I lost another about four years ago. The vet told me Heartsong is pregnant. I'll be damned if any virus is going to hurt her or her foal," he said vehemently.

Knowing that all his horses were up for sale, Rafe hadn't so much as hinted to Angela that he still had hopes that he could rescue his property from bankruptcy. She'd thought he'd come to terms emotionally with the twist of fate. Now she realized he'd been pretending to her that he didn't feel the pain. Her heart went out to him again.

"When was the last time you had anything to eat?"

Without glancing at her, he replied, "I don't remember."

"That's what I thought," she said and stood up. "I'll be back."

Rafe cooed to Heartsong while stroking her neck and chest. He didn't hear Angela's last comment nor was he aware she'd left. He only worried about his favorite mare.

Nine

Stumbling over the muddy gravel on her way to the ranch house, Angela was startled every time a lightning bolt streaked across the sky and the thunder boomed in the distance. No matter what her age, she didn't think she'd ever overcome her fear of storms.

The back door to the kitchen was unlocked, but because the electricity was still out, she nearly fell into the room. Groping around in the darkness she managed to find the fat pillar candle she remembered from her first visit to the ranch. Systematically going through the drawers from one end of the kitchen to the other, she eventually found a box of matches and lit the candle.

With a small puddle of illumination, Angela assessed the contents of the pantry and refrigerator and found both lacking in just about everything she needed to make an adequate meal. This was more evidence that things for

Rafe were worse than she feared. She hoped it was just that he was a lousy cook.

Blessedly, the stove was gas. Though it was new and required an electric ignitor, she was still able to light the burner with a match.

Remembering the small row of vegetables in the garden just outside the door, she put on her raincoat again and braved the storm. Luckily, she found winter spinach, a pumpkin and a tall sprig of rosemary.

Back inside the kitchen, she sliced several cloves of garlic, browned them in olive oil and would later brown the spinach in the oil. She made hot pumpkin soup and pan-grilled the small veal chop she'd found wrapped in butcher's paper in the meat drawer. Finding a large, old apple basket, she placed the food, silverware and napkins inside the basket along with glasses, a corkscrew and a bottle of red wine from the wine cellar.

In the hour she'd been inside the house, the rain had stopped but the thunder rolled in the distance promising yet another onslaught of storms.

Lying next to Heartsong, Rafe continued to soothe the horse with an incessant chanting Angela knew was meant to heal. During the time she'd been gone, Heartsong's lungs had lost a good deal of their raspiness. She was no longer moaning and appeared to be breathing more easily. Not realizing until now how truly worried she'd been, Angela felt her anxieties slip away. Heartsong was going to live!

Quietly, she carried the basket nearer to Rafe, then knelt and began preparing their dinner.

Sniffing the pungent garlic, both man and horse lifted their heads. Angela offered a small handful of the cooked spinach to the mare who licked her hand clean. Angela smiled when she saw the gleam in Heartsong's eyes. "She *is* feeling better."

Heartsong turned her head to the apple basket, nudging Angela with her snout. "Isn't that funny? She's so much like Rebel it's amazing. He's always ravenous when he recovers from a cold."

Startled to find the mare curious about the contents of the apple basket, Rafe quickly sat up. "She never acts like this toward strangers. She must like you." He patted her snout. "Are you hungry, girl?" Then he realized Heartsong was noticeably cooler. She'd stopped sweating through her eyes. He peered deeply into Heartsong's brown eyes. "I think you're doing much better, aren'tcha?" Rafe nuzzled the mare's neck with his nose.

Turning to Angela, Rafe smiled for the first time in days. "Guess I'll never know if it was the antibiotics, my herb concoction or you being here that brought her around."

"Maybe it was a bit of all three," Angela said placing a large dollop of spinach on a plate for him.

"Maybe," Rafe answered and took the plate Angela offered him. Ravenously, he devoured his meal in minutes. He pulled the wine out of the basket. "Good choice," he said turning the corkscrew into the cork and pulling it out.

"I wasn't sure, since the labels are hard to read on some of them. This one didn't have a label. I thought you would have labeled the most important wines."

Rafe poured out a glass for Angela and one for himself. He tapped the rim of her glass with the rim of his own. "I have a lot to teach you about wines," he said. "This one was made before I was born."

"Should we drink it?" Angela stared uneasily at the

wine. "How long before you were born?" she asked hesitantly.

"About a hundred years." He sipped the wine and swirled it in his mouth.

Her hand flew to her forehead. "Then this must be worth—"

He spat the wine out. "A lot. But only for sentimental reasons. Once you taste it, you'll understand."

Angela sipped the wine. "It's vinegar!"

"Most of the bottles are. There's no real way of knowing until they're opened, then, once opened, they're worthless."

Angela's eyes were downcast at the glass of wine. "Oh, I was hoping—"

"For a miracle? I'm fresh out." Rafe glanced around the barn as if reluctant to tell her the truth. "I had a vintner examine the wines. He told me they are worthless. That's why I haven't tried to sell them."

Looking forlornly at Heartsong, Angela said, "I wish you could, then you could keep Heartsong, Rising Star and the others. Even the ranch."

Agony streaked across Rafe's blue eyes. He stood instantly and walked away from her to stand at the open barn door. "I learned a long time ago not to be sentimentally attached to anything…anybody. This is a working ranch. I raise horses and sell them. Just like my father and grandfather. Cattle are meant to be taken to slaughter. None of what I own is worth a nickel more than what I can get at the going market price. I need Heartsong alive because she can bring me several thousand that will help get me through another season. Maybe by then this mess with my company will be cleared up and I can resume my projects."

Angela had not seen this brutally analytical side of

Rafe. He'd been oddly cool yet humorous the morning after they'd made love, but nothing he'd said then prepared her for what she was hearing.

"I've sent out feelers to the top breeders in Tennessee and Kentucky for Rising Star and for Heartsong. The fact that she's pregnant is even better."

"You've stayed with her all day and night because she'll bring a good price?"

"That's right," he glanced back at Angela over his shoulder.

When she looked him in the eyes, he quickly turned back and watched as the clouds opened up again. The rain pummeled the earth nearly drowning out the sound of his voice.

"It's more than a tough world out there, Angela. It's a killer. There's no such thing as competition anymore, it's survival of the smartest and the fastest. Without a touch of larceny, you'll never make it. I found that out. These days, good guys wear black hats."

Angela was shocked at his bitterness. Only moments ago she was ready to give her heart completely to him, but now he was telling her to keep her distance because that was exactly what he was doing.

Rafe stared at the brilliant spasms of light that severed the black sky. Thunder cracked, then boomed and rolled into the distance. Angela hugged herself wondering what frightened her more, the storm or Rafe's detached attitude.

I thought you were one of the good guys. "I don't believe that. I won't believe that."

He chuckled as he tossed his sour wine into the rain. "You're too much of a romantic."

"My friends have accused me of that many times, but I don't care. Lots of people have integrity and loyalty."

"Yeah? Well, they're fools." *I was.*

"Then I'm a fool," Angela retorted.

Rafe spun around and in three strides he stood next to her. Grabbing her arm, he pulled her up next to him. His eyes were dangerously cold as he looked at her and his mouth was thinned by anger. "You haven't got a clue what it's like to be made a fool of. I can read people better than most and I know you. I know you think you've been through some tough times, rough relationships but you've been spared a great deal, my dear. You've never stared into the jaws of the devil. Believe me, I have. I know what it's like to lose everything...I'm still learning."

His eyes held the same kind of intensity she'd seen before. It both frightened her and compelled her to want to push him further to more self-revelation. When Rafe was like this she could feel his life force surging through his body. His mind, heart and body were on fire. He was the kind of man who a hundred years ago would have been called a zealot, an idealist. He was the kind of man who made decisions and stuck by them. For some reason he didn't want to believe in his own goodness right now. It was as if he was forcing himself to be angry with the world in order to fight for his own sanity. If only she could teach him how to temper himself. She believed she was right in that there was no one to help him balance his life. If he would only trust her enough to let her in...

"Learning doesn't always mean losing. Maybe I should be your teacher," she challenged him as she placed her hand on his nape and pulled his mouth to hers.

Gently tender at first, Angela had intended the kiss to be soul healing. She wanted him to trust her enough to one day reveal his past to her. Rafe had other ideas.

He needed a release for his pent-up passion and pain. Though his kiss was forceful, it was not angry or hurtful.

It was from his kisses that Angela knew him best. Rafe could talk up a defiant storm all he wanted, but she knew the moment her lips touched his, the kind of man he was. She would bet her life on it.

Devouring her mouth with his he told her that he needed her sweetness to survive. Thrusting his tongue deep into her interior, meeting the satiny walls that gave him safe haven, he drank her compassion.

His arms encircled her like a vise, pressing her breasts into his chest, her pelvis into his. The muscles in his arms tightened keeping her locked against him. He wanted her and there was no second-guessing about it.

But for what? And for how long? Nagging her incessantly, Angela's intuition made her uneasy. Was she leaping with faith when she ought to be using caution? Rafe had called her a fool. Perhaps she was. But Angela was also a risk-taker. She'd been conservative about everything in her education and career, but Rafe was the ultimate challenge.

He'd been deeply hurt and he was trying to tell her he was never going to risk his heart again. Angela believed he only *thought* he'd been in love before. To her mind it just wasn't possible for a person to experience this all-consuming kind of passion with anyone but one's soul mate.

Desire careened through Angela's body like a juggernaut. Spinning out of control, her mind released her body. She clung to him, demanding her needs be fulfilled. She urged his tongue to take more of her. She wanted to give him everything she had, if only he would ask.

"Is it possible for a man to want a woman as much as I want you?" he asked breathlessly as he slanted his mouth over hers once again.

Anything is possible, Angela wanted to believe. "Yes. I want you more than you could ever know."

Kissing Rafe created more electricity inside Angela than the storm outside. She knew he deliberately used his lips and tongue to excite her and bring her to a point of near delirium. The heat from his body drove away the winter-night chill, keeping her warm. Hungrily he consumed every breath she took. Holding her head between his splayed fingers he opened his mouth wider, taking her in.

"I can't get enough of you," he groaned.

He covered her face with dozens of branding kisses. Not content with such a small territory, he traveled to her neck. Placing an intensely possessive kiss at the base of her throat, Rafe cradled her neck in the crook of his arm as he buried his face in the valley between her breasts.

Lunging his hand beneath the lapel of her silk jacket, he gently grasped a soft globe of flesh and brought it to his mouth. Rapaciously he licked and teased every inch of her breast until she moaned.

"You're mine now," he whispered.

"All yours," she replied, surrendering to him.

Angela couldn't control her thoughts or her body any longer. She not only wanted, she needed him inside her. Her body ached, pulsed for him in the same way her heart yearned to hear him admit that he loved her.

More than anything, Angela wanted him to tell her. Convinced he was still fighting himself by not voicing his desire, she believed the only way to bring out his true feelings was to show him she was more courageous than he.

Cupping her own breast with her hand, she urged him to continue his plunder. Rafe was happy to oblige.

"You do want me, don't you, Rafe?"

"Yes."

"Then take me. All of me. Now."

Suddenly, Rafe stopped his sexual play and lifted his head to look in her eyes. "What are you saying?"

"That I want you as much as you want me," she answered honestly. *That I'm in love with you as much as you're in love with me...if you'd ever admit it to yourself.*

In the lantern's light, Angela's passion cooled as she watched his smoky blue eyes turn brittle gray. Something she'd said had turned his ardor ice cold. But what could it be? It wasn't as if this was the first time for either of them. They knew the touch, heat and texture of each other's bodies only too well. What could have come over him?

Slowly, Rafe straightened up and gently dropped his hands from her body.

"What's the matter?" Angela asked stunned at his reaction.

"This isn't the time or place. I think it best you leave, Angela."

"This isn't...? Rafe Whitten, you make no sense at all."

"I'm making perfect sense. Heartsong was practically on her deathbed..."

"Now you just wait a minute," she retorted. "The operative word here is 'was.' She's just fine now. You have no excuse for making me feel all the things I'm feeling and then drop me cold. Unless you're simply a selfish bastard!"

Rafe's nostrils flared angrily at her attack. Through clenched teeth he said, "That I am. You should leave."

Not believing her ears, Angela's eyes narrowed in order to shoot him with a laser-intense gaze. But all she asked was, "Why?"

his mouth over hers purposefully sending a new rush of shock waves through her and himself. He felt a rash of goose bumps rise on her flesh. It was a good sign.

"Come with me," he said sweetly, pressing a tender kiss on her temple.

He took her hand and they walked to the open barn door and found the storm had passed. The cloudless indigo sky was studded with glowing galaxies. The full moon lit their way into the still dark house.

Angela wanted always to remember the timeless feeling she'd felt that night as their idyll began.

Ten

Swagging the front, side and rear porches of Rafe's ranch house with fresh pine boughs, Angela began a week-long project of making the house look like a Currier and Ives Christmas card. Filling old baskets she'd found in the barn with pine sprays and pine cones, she tied each one with enormous red bows. At a country fruit market she bought a peck of red apples to decorate the pine garland on the staircase banister. At a nursery near her townhouse, she discovered a dozen discounted poinsettias which she intended to repot in the Victorian urns on the front porch.

Rafe took Angela to the attic, where they found battered old furniture, trunks, chipped pitcher and bowl sets and fractured picture frames.

"Isn't it wonderful, Rafe?" Angela's voice hummed with excitement as she flitted from old hat boxes to dusty wooden crates.

"This is junk, Angela," Rafe cautioned.

"This is treasure. It just needs a little imagination, is all."

"You've already got the house looking like it did when my mother was alive. She did all these kinds of wonderful things," he said putting his arms around her waist and nuzzling her neck. "The holidays have been such a lonely time for me, so I never bothered with all the folderol. I'm afraid I don't have much to decorate a tree with."

Lifting her hand to his cheek, she said, "It's been that way for me, too, without a family. This year will be different. This year we have each other."

His gentle kiss was his only reply. "So, you think there's hope here?" he asked, looking around the dirty attic.

Though disappointed he didn't validate his feelings about her, Angela was undaunted. He would come around in time, she thought. "A great deal of hope," she said brightly and went back to scrounging through the crates and boxes.

"Guess I might as well dig with you."

During the ensuing half hour Rafe found his old baby clothes, an entire box filled with photographs of his ancestors he'd never seen, several hundred leatherbound books and, wonder of all wonders, Christmas ornaments from his own childhood and a dusty but pretty old pine-cone wreath.

"I'll hang this on the front door. It'll be perfect."

"Great," she said. "I'll make the bow for it. I've got plenty of tree lights at my house. We'll string cranberries and popcorn and it'll be a real old-fashioned Christmas."

"I guess this means you want me to put up a tree," he said.

"Oh, didn't I mention that?" she asked playfully.

He chuckled along with her. "I've seen that little vixen

look you get when your mind starts whirling. I have a feeling I have a great deal of work ahead of me."

Smiling, she nodded. "Uh-huh. Starting with sanding and painting these little chairs."

"What for? No one can sit in them. The wood is so old and rotted they'd crumble with any weight at all."

"Silly. I don't intend to *use* them as chairs."

Rafe was baffled. "Okay, I give." He flung up his hands.

"I'm going to tie bows around the backs and stack fake wrapped packages on them and put them on either side of the front door. They're perfect for the pictures."

"Pictures? What pictures?"

"Oops! Guess I didn't tell you." She gnawed her lower lip thoughtfully. "Remember when I told you that I thought it would be best to advertise in places like New York and Los Angeles? Well, to get a quick sale I need to push a bit harder. I've still got time to make the Valentine's edition of two magazines. A farm can be so romantic. Granted we don't have snow, but in February, East Coast buyers are trying to get away from the cold. They'll be looking for a place that gives them a warm and fuzzy feeling inside. That's the buyer we want and nothing creates nostalgia like Christmas."

Gleaming with admiration, Rafe's eyes were crystal blue when he looked at her. "I'm impressed. You've really put some thought into all this."

"Yes, I have. Besides, I love doing this kind of thing…making homes out of houses."

"And you do it well."

"Thank you. Now, if we're going to make that deadline, we've got a lot of work ahead of us."

He bowed theatrically. "I'm at your service. Do with

me what you will.''

Laughing she thought, Don't I wish!

Because the interior of the house was virtually devoid of furnishings now that Rafe had sold off the best pieces, Angela insisted they drag nearly everything down from the attic. She scrubbed the old trunks, polished the brass hardware till it gleamed, then filled them with old quilts, blankets and sheets and put one in each bedroom. She glued an old rocker's back together, washed it with wood soap and put it in the living room with a lacy shawl draped over the worst of the cracked slats.

Old pitchers were filled with magnolia leaves and fruit and put in the kitchen and bathrooms. She gilded the broken mirror frames, tossed out the cracked glass and stretched Victorian lace hand towels across the frames and hung them on the walls in the dining room. Without a dining-room table and chairs, Angela decided to turn the room into an old Victorian library. The one remaining writing desk in the attic was minus two legs. Rafe volunteered to saw off the remaining two and then replaced all four legs with stacks of old books they'd found in the attic. They lined the shelves of an old breakfront with books and Rafe erected slat-and-brick ''bookshelves'' between the tall beveled glass windows. Angela festooned the rest of the room with pine and magnolia boughs she cut from trees on the property.

On Saturday evening, Rafe saddled Rising Star and Honey Biscuit, a pretty caramel-and-ivory two-year-old mare he'd promised to a rancher in Abilene. He explained that the owner wanted delivery the third of January after returning from a family Christmas vacation in Colorado.

Helping Angela into the saddle, Rafe said, ''I think I know where we'll find a perfect tree to decorate. We can haul it back Indian-style with this old blanket and ropes.

While we're out this way, I want to show you a special place of mine.''

''What kind of place?'' Angela asked placing her booted foot in the stirrup.

Swinging onto Rising Star's back, Rafe smiled. ''It's a secret. You wouldn't want to spoil the surprise would you?''

''Wouldn't dream of it,'' she bantered.

Gazing at her curiously, he asked, ''It's odd you say it that way. I call it my 'dreaming place.'''

It's not odd, Rafe. It's destiny. ''I can't wait to see it.''

''You sure that saddle is tight enough? Maybe I should raise the stirrups a bit.''

''They're fine, Rafe. I've been riding since I was a kid.'' *After all, I didn't come by my dreams of cowboy heroes just from the movies.*

''Really?'' He opened the corral gate and then closed it after them.

''I haven't told you but I was brought up on a ranch much like this near San Antonio. We didn't have all these lovely trees, but my grandfather was a cattle rancher and we lived in the same house all my life until my parents were killed in an airplane crash.''

''How old were you again?''

''Eighteen,'' she answered without emotion, as if giving the details of someone else's life. How strange it was to think of it all now from this distance of time and space, she thought. ''Since I was the only child, I had to sell the cattle and the ranch myself.''

''Couldn't you have kept it? Worked it yourself?''

''I was capable, but my father had mortgaged the property to the hilt. I couldn't pay off his loans.''

''This is incredible. Our lives are so parallel. We've

both been through the same kinds of situations, just at different times in our lives."

"I noticed that the first day I saw this ranch. I know how you've been forced to detach yourself from your family memories in order to survive. I had to do the same. Fortunately for me, I was able to keep all the furnishings and family heirlooms. I suppose I'm guilty of pretending I still have them near me."

"But you were so young to go through all that."

Aware of the compassion in his voice, she turned her face to him. "It wasn't nearly as bad as what you're facing. You'll have nothing left...."

Tearing his eyes from hers, he looked off to the sunset. A severely determined expression covered his face. "Did you ever think that maybe it's our fate to start all over again? That perhaps we're supposed to create new legacies?"

Smiling, she thought, *And who would have thought you'd have the heart of a poet?* "Something like that."

Snapping out of his reverie, he said, "Since you know how to ride, I'll race you to the dreaming place."

"That's not fair, you know where you're going."

With only the lightest tap of his stirrups, Rafe urged Rising Star from a trot to a gallop. "I know! That way I'll win!" He tore off toward the southwest.

"Come on, Honey Biscuit! We can't let a man beat us!" Angela gave the horse's flank a light slap and they were off, gaining ground faster than she'd thought possible.

Honey Biscuit was younger than Rising Star and though her legs weren't as long, she made up for her shortcomings with sheer force of will. Angela could tell from only moments in the saddle that this horse had racing blood.

Oak and pine trees streamed past Angela as she flew

after Rafe, with Honey Biscuit only a nose behind. Though the afternoon was still quite warm, after sundown she knew she would be glad of the brightly colored Indian-print wool jacket Rafe had loaned her.

Rafe pointed to a cluster of trees in the distance indicating their destination. It was the biggest mistake he'd made.

Angela leaned over the mare's head and pressed her to run even faster. Though Rising Star matched her speed, the younger Honey Biscuit had a lighter jockey in Angela. It was all the edge she needed to win the race.

When they came to a halt by the towering pines and spreading magnolias, man, woman and horses were out of breath. Rafe jumped off his horse and bent in half at the waist to work out the kinks in his lower back. "How did you do that? I had no idea Honey Biscuit could run that fast."

"I suppose you were the jockey?" Angela asked panting.

"You think you're better at racing than I am? Forget it. I train these horses—"

Angela cut him off. "I weigh 118. How much do you weigh?"

"I get your point. And if you want to know, 195. All muscle."

"So I've noticed," she laughed. "It's just my opinion, but I think Honey Biscuit could win a Preakness or Belmont Stakes. She's got natural talent."

"I know she does. That's why I called a fella I know in Kentucky to buy her. Jack's got great stables and he's got the money to pay for her and Rising Star."

Hitting her like a blast of sobering cold wind, Angela was beginning to realize how ever-present Rafe's financial situation was on his mind.

Walking over to her, Rafe held out his hand. "Come on, I can't wait for you to see this."

Bringing the horses with them, Rafe cut through a screen of thick wild wisteria and jasmine vines. Like parting curtains, the vines opened onto a tranquil pond surrounded by thick beds of grass, lichen, ferns and moss. Huge willows tickled the water's surface with long golden fingers. Because Texas trees don't lose their leaves until a heavy frost, usually in January, a thick canopy of green stretched over the pond, keeping it cool in the summer and warmer in the winter.

Rafe untied his bedroll blanket while Angela led the horses to the water's edge for a drink.

Sitting on the blanket next to Rafe and pulling her knees under her chin, she unselfconsciously laid her head on his shoulder. "It's more than just beautiful here, it's peaceful and..." She paused, searching for the right words. "I can't describe it."

"I know. This place is something you feel and see, but can't verbally express."

"I can see why it has inspired your dreams. It's very strange but I don't feel alone here."

Of course... I'm with you.

"Ever since I can remember I've felt just that way about it. Of all the possessions, the house, the horses and every blade of grass on this land, I'll miss this place the most."

"Why?"

"Because my great-grandmother stumbled onto it one day when there was nothing here but this spring-fed pond. Back then it would dry up in the summer. She took saplings of pines, magnolia, oaks, willows and even a couple of apple trees and planted every tree you see here. When my grandmother was a young wife, she helped my great-grandmother plant all the ferns and flowers that bloom in the spring and summer. There's everything from bluebonnets to honeysuckle around here. Before I moved into the city after college, I was afraid to miss a single day here because each day was always more beautiful than the last.''

"I can only imagine," she sighed. "Tell me, what dreams did you make here?''

"Oh, the usual kid things. Silly things. Exotic travel. Becoming rich…maybe even famous for something.''

"Like what?''

Leaning back and crossing his arms behind his head, he said, "I don't know. Finding a cure for cancer, I guess. I wanted to change the world.''

From what I observe, you still do. With your telecommunications company, I mean.''

He closed his eyes for a long minute. "I had great plans. I was going to bring phone service to the Ivory Coast of Africa. Doesn't sound like much, but using this method I invented of roboted unmanned planes that would pick up satellite signals from around the world, I could literally have had instant cellular communications beamed across half the face of Africa in less than a six-month period. I called it Eagle-Tech.''

"That's brilliant. Almost like…automated homing pigeons.''

"That's right. The main reason Third-World countries remain Third World is their lack of communications. How can they adequately use new technologies when the only way they have of sending messages is by drum beats?''

Angela observed how his voice and body became animated as he explained his ideas to her. He was intensely zealous about his work and its possibility of success. Easily she realized how his invention could change the world.

Once he got the operation working in Africa, then the rest of the world would be beckoning to him to bring his technology. Rafe was more than a hero, he was a shapeshifter, as the Indians used to say. He was a man of vision.

Angela was awed.

The more he explained, the more she wished she could do something to help. How incredible it was to her that this man's ability to create new worlds halfway across the globe rested upon her talent and business savvy. The sooner she could sell this ranch, the better for so many people.

Viewing life as an intricately woven tapestry in which all men and women are the threads, and their crisscrossing paths create the fabric, had always fascinated Angela. This was the first time in her life she'd experienced the weaving at its beginning.

"I'll do everything in my power to get this sale for you, Rafe," she said.

"I have no doubt of that. I can't believe the miracles you've worked already. Even my ancestors weren't as creative as you making something out of nothing." He placed his hand on her back and pulled gently on the wool jacket so that she was lying beside him. "The house looks great."

He touched her cheek softly and gazed appreciatively into her eyes. "I want to make love to you here, Angela. I've never brought anyone here."

"Never?" She asked the question hesitantly, secretly wondering if he was telling the truth.

"Not once...ever." *Not even Cheryl.*

Am I that special to you, Rafe? Please tell me that I am. I need to know. "I'm honored."

Propping his elbow he placed his face in his hand and gazed longingly into Angela's eyes. "You're so very beautiful.'' He slipped his fingers into her hair and let its curls twine around them like silver rings. ''You do remind me of an angel.''

She pulled his hand to her mouth and kissed the inside of his palm. ''How would you know? When did you ever see an angel?''

Gliding her beneath him, he began unbuttoning the wool jacket he'd given her. ''I saw an angel looking back at me the first night we met. I still see her and she hasn't changed a bit.''

Covering her mouth with his, Rafe kissed Angela with the kind of tender passion she'd come to crave from him. Angela felt the floodgates of her heart open and wash them both with love. She wanted to tell him what was in her heart, but she knew he wasn't ready to hear it. Someone, somewhere in his past, had hurt him so deeply there was no room for tears. Sometimes she wished she knew who that person was and what they had done. Her intuition warned her not to open that Pandora's box. She might not like what she found.

Instead, she prayed for them both.

Make love to me as if you believe we'll never end. Make your dreams with me, Rafe. I'll never let you down.

Eleven

"**W**hat the hell's going on, Angela?" Randy barked in his own inimitable way as he leaned over her desk.

"Don't curse, Randy. It's Christmas Eve," Angela replied, not taking her eyes from her computer screen and competently clicking her mouse at a dizzying speed.

"I'll do whatever I please, thank you very much," he growled a bit less loudly.

"It's bad luck." Concentrating on the task at hand, she finished up the entry she was making and clicked her mouse onto the print function. She looked up at her boss and frowned. "Now, what are you talking about?"

"Look around. Does it look like Christmas Eve here? No, it doesn't. And do you know why?"

Shrugging her shoulders, she baited him. "No, I don't."

Randy's face flushed. "Because some cockamamie scheme of yours to sell this Whitten ranch has caused the biggest damn stir since the Japanese bought Houston after the oil crash.''

Waving away his arguments, Angela rose to gather her papers from the printer. She marched over to the fax machine with Randy following fast on her heels. "Can I help it that I'm brilliant? Can I help it that I'm going to wind up being your top salesperson of the year? What's your problem with all that, Randy?"

He thrust his agitated finger at the bank of secretaries taking a deluge of incoming calls. "I've got girls out there working on double-time wages because one person can't keep up with all the calls. Last night the phone recorder ran out of tape we had so many calls."

"So? Get one of those new digital things. No tapes involved," she bantered with a purposely sickeningly sweet smile. *Man, I love it when I'm right.*

"Are these people calling in because they want to buy houses? Rent apartments or condos? Ooooh, noooo! They want to buy your goofy antiques. Where can they get those rags you framed to give to Aunt Molly for Christmas? It's driving me crazy, I tell you."

She patted him patronizingly on the shoulder. "You can't fool me for one minute, Randy. Besides the four houses I've sold, I checked with Julia and she's sold two houses this past week off those calls. So has Margaret. And Ilsa? She's a *secretary* and *she* sold that awful mess in Bellaire because it 'reminded' her of a ranch house. You've been trying to dump that place for two years. So, gimme a break, Randy. I've brought in more money off that ad than these girls will ever make in a year."

"You have no idea what it costs for my overhead here…the lights, the office supplies."

Angela refused to let him dampen her holiday spirit. "You're such a fussbudget. Know what I think?"

"Spare me," he droned.

"You should give all the girls a Christmas bonus. Five hundred bucks each. Yeah, that's about right. What do you think?"

"You're crazy."

Waving the stack of papers in her hand and then sliding them onto the fax machine, she punched out a long distance number and sent the fax. "See that? That's the buyer for the West ranch I told you about. They're in Grand Cayman right now, but are flying back New Year's Day to look at the ranch. He's already sent me a thousand dollar nonrefundable check just so I won't let anyone else see the place before he gets here."

Randy's face went from wildly elated to gravity. "Grand Cayman? How much does that cost a minute on a holiday to fax?"

Angela rolled her eyes and walked away. "Go home, Randy. You need a Christmas drink. A stiff one," she laughed.

One by one, Randy went to the secretaries and informed each one to finish her call, hang up and go home. Mumbling to himself, he retreated into his office and packed his briefcase.

Just as Angela shut down her computer screen, Ilsa came over.

"What is it about you that Randy hates so much?" Ilsa asked.

"Let me count the ways," Angela laughed. "He knows I'm as good a businessperson as he is, for one. The fact that I can sell and he can't chips away at his ego daily. But the biggest factor is that he needs me, and Randy isn't the kind of guy who wants to need anyone. Least of all, me." She bent over and pulled the white plastic liner out of her wastebasket, remembering it was one of

Randy's odd rules that he wanted everyone's trash emptied before they left the office at night. Angela guessed he got a discount from the maid service if all the agents complied.

Ilsa cocked her head to the left and glanced at a still frustrated Randy in his office. "I dunno. I think he doesn't like your face." Then she burst into laughter.

"Come on, I'll walk you out," Angela said still chuckling at Ilsa's joke.

"Better yet, how about we meet Julia for a drink before going home?"

Shaking her head, Angela replied, "I can't. I promised Rafe I'd bring a turkey home for us to smoke tomorrow for Christmas. I meant to stop at the grocery before coming in to work, but I knew if I wanted to get all this information to the McIlwains by two their time in the Caymans, I'd never make it."

"So, you really think this deal will go through?"

"I'd bet my reputation on it. I sent him a video of every inch of the ranch. Tim McIlwain told me he'd fallen in love for the second time in his life. The first was his wife."

"Really? Can you imagine a man saying something so sweet?" Ilsa gushed.

"Yeah." *I can only imagine.*

"Speaking of which, we don't see much of you these days. Spending even more time with Rafe, hmm?"

Angela had never liked giving details about her love life until the relationship fell apart. That way she didn't have to hear her own words coming out of her friends' mouths especially when all she wanted was to forget the whole thing. "Yes."

"What? No details?"

"None to tell," Angela answered as they walked to their respective cars in the parking lot.

"I don't believe that. I drove by your townhouse and for the first time since I've known you, there's no tree up and no lights on the ligustrums. He must be serious to be that possessive."

Angela tossed her purse and briefcase into the back seat. "I guess he is." *He certainly doesn't like me staying in town for a single night. Rafe likes me by his side at all times. What's so wild about it all, it feels comfortable to me.*

"Are you coming in to work the day after Christmas or taking it off like most of us?"

"Taking it off," Angela said.

"Well, that's a first for you. I never thought I'd see the day when you, Miss Workaholic, took a holiday. Tell Rafe I think he's worked a miracle. Does he walk on water, too?"

"How you do go on," Angela joked in an exaggerated Southern-belle voice. "Better watch out, I may even go on a...dare I say it? Vacation?"

"Lawsie, Miss Scarlett! Will wonders never cease?" Ilsa mocked Angela's diction.

"Merry Christmas, Ilsa. And tell Julia not to worry about me. I'm just fine. I know she's not happy unless she's fidgety over something I have or haven't done."

"I will," Ilsa said, waving as she got into her car and drove off.

Angela turned into the traffic flow planning the Christmas dinner she and Rafe would share. She turned up the volume on the radio and the strains of "Silent Night" filled her head.

It was going to be a wonderful Christmas for her. For them.

Rafe was at the ranch chopping wood for their fire tonight. He'd promised to grill shrimp and tuna steaks and he'd found a bottle of white wine that had not soured. They agreed they would open their presents to each other on Christmas morning, both adamantly declaring it was nearly sacrilegious to open anything on Christmas Eve.

Knowing that Rafe had little if any money for a gift for her, she'd suggested they only give something they had made, not purchased. Stealing herself away from him long enough to create something special had been the hardest part.

Ever since their evening at his dreaming place, Rafe had been attached to her like glue. He wanted them to do everything together.

They fixed the back door together; she held the screws while he put in new hardware. They cleaned the house together, both working in the same room together until the job was completed. Then they'd move on to the next room.

From morning to night, he played her favorite romantic ballads from the twenties, thirties and forties. Humming, he'd come up to her, take her in his arms and dance "cheek to cheek" just like the song said.

Angela didn't mind paying for the groceries once she discovered Rafe was a gourmet cook. Once she tasted his orange and curry quail, she fully understood why he'd invested so much money in the kitchen. Though he was a dashing figure on horseback racing across the pasture and through tall trees, his real passion was cooking. Viciously critiquing his work, he allowed himself no room for failure. Rafe told Angela that he expected only the best from himself and nothing less would ever do.

She'd told him point-blank his culinary panache intimidated her.

"Believe me, sweetheart, I don't want you for your cooking," he'd said and then made love to her on the granite counter.

Nearly three weeks living with Rafe should have left her satiated with sex for the rest of her life, but unfortunately she wanted him as much this very minute as she had the first time.

Angela was in love. Insanely, head over heels, illogically, profusely in love with a wonderful, caring man.

Picking up her cellular phone, Angela dialed Ilsa's cellular. On the second ring it was answered.

"Hello?" Ilsa said.

"In answer to your question, Ilsa. Yes. He does walk on water."

Twelve

Rebel trotted into Rafe's bedroom, carrying a long red Christmas stocking embroidered with the Rebel flag and filled with dog treats. Being the Southern gentleman that he was, Rebel never barked unless his mistress was in danger from an intruder. He dropped the stocking on the bare floor with a thud, sat back on his haunches and breathed heavily until Angela's eyes opened.

"Good morning, boy," Angela reached out her hand to pet him. "I see you've already decided it's time to open presents, huh?"

Rebel laid his head on the pillow next to Angela as she continued to caress him.

Rafe rose slowly onto his elbows and looked over at Rebel. "You both make quite a happy scene. Merry Christmas," he leaned over to kiss Angela.

"Merry Christmas," *darling,* Angela wanted to say.

"I'll make the coffee while you turn on the tree lights,"

he suggested, rolling out of bed and donning a navy velour robe.

Padding across the floor, Angela tied a knot in her white terry-cloth robe, with Rebel following closely behind carrying his stocking down the stairs.

It was not quite dawn as Angela plugged in the lights illuminating the room with a soft hue. Letting Rebel out the front door for his early morning "stroll," she turned back to the tree and noticed two packages wrapped in brown paper and tied up with string, to which Rafe had attached a sprig of holly.

"Hey, I thought we were only giving one gift," she yelled out to the kitchen.

"We are," Rafe replied walking into the room. He handed her a cup of steaming coffee. "One for you. One for Rebel."

"I didn't see any tags," she replied a bit sheepishly.

"I didn't make any."

"I've noticed you have an organizational problem," she teased.

"That's absolutely not true. I know where everything is around here." Tapping his temple, he said, "I keep very good records up here."

"I understand that, but that kind of filing system makes it difficult for everyone else but you." She walked over to the tree and picked up a prettily wrapped box. "That's why I made you this."

Smiling, Rafe sat down on the floor Indian-style and opened his gift. After carefully removing the huge gold bow, he ripped through the paper like a child. He flung the box top down and dug through the white tissue paper and found large gummed labels printed with "West Wines of Waller County" across the top. In the four corners were colorful motifs of grape clusters and vines wound around a pair of horseshoes.

"I thought we agreed to make our gifts."

"I did...on the computer," she beamed. "Do you like them?"

"I love 'em! We'll put them on this afternoon while I smoke the turkey," he said happily as he pulled her down to the floor and kissed her. Encircling her with his arms he playfully pinned her to the floor. He smoothed back a handful of silver hair. "You're a pretty special lady, Angela Morton."

She gazed up at him lovingly. "You're the special one. There aren't many men like you left in the world, Rafe Whitten."

As always, his kiss excited her, yet was deeply comforting. "Now, it's your turn. The small one is for Rebel."

"Omigosh!" She struggled away from Rafe's possessive hold. "I left him outside." Racing to the door, she yanked it open and found Rebel standing patiently on the other side. As Rebel walked inside, Angela turned to Rafe. "His manners are so impeccable he wouldn't dare interrupt us by scratching on a door."

"How did you teach him that?" Rafe asked holding out his gift for the dog.

"I didn't. It's breeding, pure and simple." She sat next to Rafe and opened the package. Inside was a small wooden handcarved name tag. "You didn't make this yourself."

"I certainly did," Rafe said proudly. "I learned to whittle when I was eight. I'm no artist, but I get my point across."

"I think it's very good," Angela said hooking the tag onto Rebel's collar. "Say thank you to Rafe," she in-

structed Rebel who immediately pounced on Rafe and
licked his nose.

Laughing at the sight of her dog nearly pinning Rafe
to the floor, she said, "I *did* teach him how to properly
give thanks."

Satisfied that he'd done his gentlemanly duty, Rebel left
Rafe alone and sauntered off to the kitchen for his water
and food.

"Your turn," Rafe said to Angela and gave her the
larger box of the two.

She untied the string and after the brown paper fell
away, she lifted the lid and pulled the crumpled newspa-
per aside to reveal a wooden oval plaque in which an
angel's face and wings had been carved. Joyous tears
filled Angela's eyes as she said, "This is the most beautiful gift I've ever received," she whispered.

Smiling, Rafe placed his hand over hers. "I'm not tal-
ented enough to capture your real essence, but I did the
best I could."

"It's uncannily like myself. I think you underestimate
your ability. Why, my nose and mouth are exact."

"I know, but it's the eyes I couldn't possibly dupli-
cate," he said in hushed tones, moving closer to her.

"When did you do this? I never knew..."

"During the day while you were at work mostly. I con-
fess I did slip out of bed at night while you were sleeping
to finish it up. I put the finishing touches on it a couple
hours ago."

"You're incredible." *Maybe you do love me. I will
treasure this all my life.*

Rafe leaned over to kiss her. "I guess I got into the
Christmas spirit more than I'd thought. Thank you for
giving that to me."

Holding the plaque next to her chest, Angela felt herself

surrender to his touch. No matter how many times Rafe had kissed her, it was never enough. It would never be enough. She'd become like one of those silly refrains in a love song, addicted to love. She remembered laughing at girlfriends who'd said they'd made fools of themselves over a man. Angela had done some stupid things in the past for the sake of a relationship, but she'd always known she could get out when she'd tired of the situation.

Rafe was different. He was buried so deep in her heart she knew he'd always be a part of her.

As his kiss became more passionate, igniting both their desires, Angela realized the carving she held was her talisman of the truth.

Rafe *must* love her to spend so many hours thinking about her every curve and angle. He *had* to have filled his mind with memories of their most intimate moments. Still, something stopped him from declaring his feelings for her, even on Christmas morning.

Disappointed that Rafe chose to keep himself distant from her, Angela refused to give up hope. Though it seemed impossible to her, his kiss became more possessive than ever. He held her close to his chest and plunged his tongue into her mouth taking what he wanted. His arms felt like steel bands as he cradled her head in his hand, kissing her with increased intensity. She knew he wouldn't waste time going upstairs. His desire had plummeted over the edge of reason.

Panting like an animal running at breakneck speed, Rafe untied the sash on Angela's robe. She lowered the plaque and let it rest on the floor. Puddling around her, the white robe revealed her flawless alabaster skin. Rafe caressed her neck, throat and breasts reverently, as if she were fine porcelain.

"I've never known anyone could be so beautiful. So

utterly perfect," he whispered, tearing his eyes from hers to gaze at her breast. Taking her flesh in his hand and gently cupping the round globe, he slowly brought her nipple to his lips.

Nibbling the bud, he sent intense waves of heat through her body. Angela could hear her heart banging against her chest with his first taste. Her breathing sounded like a metronome in quarter-time. As his hand caressed her softly rounded abdomen the anticipation of its final destination increased her heartbeat. She held her breath as she waited impatiently for his fingers to enter her. Expelling a rush of hot air, she felt him fill her, stretch her walls and stroke her until her body arched onto him.

"Always ready for me, aren't you, Angela?" he asked in a husky sensual voice.

"Yes, Rafe," she whispered as she felt the brush of his robe against her skin as it fell away from his body.

Teasing her aching bud, Rafe intensified Angela's need. He clamped his mouth on hers taking her tongue at the same moment as he pushed deep inside her. "Tell me you're mine, Angela," he demanded hoarsely.

"I...am..." she replied, barely able to think or speak.

"Tell me," he demanded even more possessively.

"I'm yours," she whispered as she felt herself spinning out of control. Unbelievably, she was climaxing already. Clamping her arms around him, then grabbing his buttocks she pushed him even more deeply inside her. She wanted to believe with all her heart that he was just as much hers as she was his. With his body Rafe told her that he wanted, needed and craved her. She hoped he understood that she felt the same.

Of all the days, of all their times together, she wanted him to give her the only Christmas gift she would ever want or need. She wanted his love.

Screaming with pleasure, Angela buried her face in the hollow of Rafe's shoulder. She felt completely exhausted, but Rafe continued to stroke her. His hips drove into her, deliciously stretching her, making her pulse all over again in a new wave of passion.

"Take me, Angel."

Slowly, she opened her eyes and found him looking so deeply into her, his gaze nearly hurt.

He pushed himself deeper. She could feel each rhythmic rush of blood as it coursed through his body to the end of his shaft. She felt her walls beat in time with him. They were truly one entity.

His voice was barely an audible rasp when he spoke, overwhelmed with sexual need. "See me, Angel? See me take you with my eyes. Feel me inside you. You're mine."

Blinking away the emotional tears in her eyes, Angela watched as Rafe's lids fell halfway over his eyes as he shivered.

"Oh, Angel, baby, you're mine...."

"Yes, Rafe, I am," she replied as she arched into him. She felt as if she'd been catapulted to heaven. Not once, not even twice—three times. She couldn't breathe, couldn't see and couldn't feel anything except ecstasy.

Clinging to him on her descent back to consciousness, Angela wanted only to express her joy. But she couldn't find the words.

Rafe pulled her to him, kissed her forehead and said, "Merry Christmas, Angela. You make me happy."

Thirteen

Angela and Rafe's romantic idyll was broken by Tim and Rita McIlwain's arrival on January fifth.

"Sorry, we didn't get here as planned," Tim said shaking Rafe's hand and then introducing his petite, thirty-something, dark-haired wife to Angela and Rafe. "We had unexpected news that delayed our return nearly a week."

"Nothing bad, I hope," Angela said to Rita.

Rita blushed and looked at her husband, who nodded back, smiling. "I became ill just after Christmas. I didn't know about these things," she stumbled quietly as she chose her words. "This being, well, we were trying…you know…"

Tim slipped his arm around Rita's shoulder. "Well, you see, we're pregnant!" He announced proudly.

Rita beamed like the sun while Angela shook her hand.

"That's wonderful," Angela said enthusiastically. She

noticed that Rafe smiled, but his eyes did not sparkle the way she'd come to know they did when he was truly excited about something. She chalked it up to the fact that Rafe was usually a bit standoffish with strangers.

"Congratulations, Tim," Rafe said politely.

"Thanks. You can see now why this place is even more important to us than before. With a family on the way, our home has to be just right."

Angela detected a note of warning in Tim's words—that if Rita or he didn't feel absolutely "right" about every blade of grass on the ranch, nothing would sway them to buy. Angela surmised that Tim and Rita wouldn't be as easy a sale as she'd thought. This pregnancy had thrown an entirely new light on everything.

Normally, Angela wouldn't allow an owner to be present during a showing, but in Rafe's case all the rules had been thrown out the door from the day she'd begun his ad campaign. Because Rafe was an expert on the ranch, she let him tell his favorite family stories rather than pointing out the fact that the barn could use some new hardware, hinges and even a new second-level fan/circulation system.

Angela made certain Rita was aware of extra safety features around the house, barn and stables that would help her once the baby began toddling around—like the double lock on the corral gate, the fact that the pond was a considerable distance from the house, and the porch railing rungs, which were so close together that no child could get his head stuck between them, or fall through. She pointed out that the floorboards on the porch were smooth and level. There would be no falls, scratches or splinters.

Tim and Rita were classic home buyers, showing little emotion as they made their way around the property, but

Angela had been in the business for too long not to pick up on the winks, nudges and quick nods they used to signal their approval to the other.

However, very little was said between them until they walked into the house through the front door. Rita took one look at Angela's old-fashioned tree and burst into tears.

"That's the most beautiful tree I've ever seen. I've always, always wanted a country-looking tree," she sniffed as she turned to Angela who handed her a clean tissue from her pocket. "I was raised in New York and my mother was quite uncreative. For the longest time I thought all Christmas trees had red satin balls and white plastic bells. Last year, Tim and I were on our honeymoon and this year we were in Cayman, so we've yet to have a tree."

Tim put his arm around his wife. "I doubt the tree is part of the house, darling."

Angela smiled charmingly. "I took some liberties decorating the ranch house for the ads my company photographed out here. We've had great response, but like I told Tim, you have first peek." She paused only momentarily and then said, "Let me show you the kitchen, which I think is just wonderful for preparing all those large family holiday dinners you'll be serving. A hundred years ago it might have been quaint to bake in a woodburning stove, but today with small children you'll be using a microwave...a lot."

Everyone followed Angela into the kitchen.

Rafe couldn't help the proud smile on his lips as he listened to Angela professionally and honestly guide Tim and Rita through his house. He was amazed at the way she'd remembered the tiniest details from his stories. Not until they reached the master bedroom, did she turn to

Rafe and ask him to explain the poignant family history regarding the carved rice bed.

Tim and Rita were enraptured with his story. It was like smoothing icing on the cake. He'd barely gotten his last words out when Rita turned to Tim.

"Darling, it's perfect."

"Are you sure?"

Smiling sheepishly, she replied, "Yes. Very sure. I want to raise our children here."

Tim looked at Angela and said, "I guess you and I have some talking to do."

"It seems so," she replied happily.

"It's been a long day for Rita and I'd like to get her back to our apartment and let her rest. Will it be all right if I meet you at your office, say, in two hours?"

"That would be fine. I'll be going back shortly and again, I want to thank you for allowing Mr. Whitten to be present."

"Oh, I wouldn't have missed it for the world," Rita gushed, taking Rafe's hand. "I know this must be difficult for you to leave this land you so clearly cherish. Please know that we would welcome a visit from you anytime."

"Darling, we haven't bought the property yet," Tim warned.

"Oh, pooh. This bargaining thing is just a formality. They know as well as we do that, well, with the baby coming, we need this ranch now. It's our turn," Rita said happily.

"Yes, dear," Tim said and turned to Rafe and shook his hand. "I'll be in touch."

"Great," Rafe replied a bit hollowly and then watched as the McIlwains drove away. With vacant eyes he glanced at Angela. "Guess you better be going."

She put her hand affectionately on his sleeve. "I can stay for a bit if you'd like."

"No, I'd rather you didn't. I think I'll take Rising Star out for a ride."

"I understand," she replied, hoping to comfort him.

Rafe's eyes turned stormy as he ground his jaw. "I know you think you do, but it's different for a man. I lost my ancestors' legacy to me. I should have been smarter; known better. I should have done a thousand and one things differently in my life," he growled bitterly. *Not the least of which was Cheryl.*

Angela hadn't seen Rafe this angry since the first day she'd come to the ranch to list it. It was if all their days since then had never existed. He'd brought her into the circle of his warmth and now had shut her out. She felt used. Mostly, she was afraid she'd never find her way back in again.

"Please don't beat yourself up over things that were beyond your control."

His lips curled into a sneer. "Don't hand out platitudes about something you don't know about."

"But you told me your partner…" she began but he cut her off.

"I know exactly what I told you. Now, I'm telling you I want to be left alone."

"Rafe, please," she put her hand on his back refusing to allow him to treat her like a stranger. "It's me, Angela."

Her touch was like a cool, calming wind, he thought. "I'm sorry. I guess I've been more torn up about this than I'd realized. For a while there I actually forgot about my problems, thanks to you." He gazed into her searching brown eyes. "I'll be fine. You go back and dicker with Tim and make him happy and let me know what he says."

Smiling, she placed a kiss on his cheek. "Any last instructions?"

He chuckled sarcastically to himself. "Yeah, don't blow the deal. I'd like to agree on something tonight and sign the papers immediately so they can get their financing handled as quickly as possible."

"Okay," she replied and squeezed his hand before walking over to her car. She turned around to wave goodbye, but Rafe had already gone through the corral gate. He was too far away to hear.

Tim made a fair counteroffer Rafe did not refuse. Within twenty-four hours Angela had all original copies signed and Tim had contacted his banker. Angela went back to her townhouse to get her mail, feed Rebel and check her personal messages. She was home no more than forty minutes when Julia called to congratulate her.

"Thanks, Julia. I can't tell you how excited I am. Even though I didn't pull off the sale by the end of the year, it's a heck of a way to start the New Year. What did Randy say when he came back?"

Laughing, Julia said, "He's appopleptic. He'd love not to pay you the bonus he promised. Lord! What a tightwad that man is! How about I come over and we go out for a quick drink before you head off into the sunset tonight?"

"Sounds great. Actually, I'm not sure if I'll be going out to the ranch tonight."

"Oops! Lover's quarrel?" Julia inquired.

"No. Rafe is quite upset about the sale. And rightly so. I've been where he's at and it's not fun nor pretty. I get the feeling he wants to be alone."

"A guy thing, huh?"

"A Rafe thing anyway," Angela replied with a sigh.

Julia paused before asking, "Seems to me at a time like

this he'd want the woman he loves to be with him. How does that make you feel, Angela?''

"Feel?" Angela remembered their lovemaking on Christmas. She'd fallen so deeply in love with him she thought he certainly *must* be in love with her. Apparently, she'd been very wrong. The thought devastated her.

"I feel as if the bottom is quickly falling out of my world, Julia," Angela replied as self-pitying tears flooded her eyes and her stomach lurched. Then her stomach lurched again. She slammed her hand over her mouth. She took a deep breath.

"I feel I'm going to be very, very sick," Angela cried, dropped the receiver and dashed to the bathroom.

"Angela? Are you all right? What the heck is going on over there? Angela? Angela? I'm coming right over!"

Julia pressed a cold compress to Angela's forehead. "Here, hold this while I check the results."

"This is ridiculous," Angela sighed heavily.

"No, this is blue," Julia showed the litmus paper to Angela who immediately sat bolt upright on the couch.

"Impossible!" Angela stared at the blue paper that proved the test result was positive. "I can't be pregnant."

Julia patted her leg. "These things can be wrong sometimes."

Frowning, Angela sank her face in her hand. "We've done the damn thing four times!"

Julia gathered up the box, printed instructions and the rest and threw them in the trash compactor in the kitchen. Walking back into the living room she said, "Look, this can't be so terrible. Your cowboy hero clearly loves you even if he hasn't said so. Sometimes, guys need a little push."

Rolling her eyes Angela groaned, "But this is a shove

into the gorge. He didn't bargain for anything like this and besides, I want to know he loves me first before I tell him he's going to be a father. I wanted everything to be so right between us," she sobbed wiping her tears away with her fingertips. *How can this be happening? I took the pill every day... Except for that first night here in my townhouse. I hadn't known he was coming over. I missed my prescription for...oh, my God...four days. How could I be so busy that I didn't stop at the pharmacy?*

Julia sat next to Angela and hugged her. "Don't do this to yourself, Angela. You've gotten yourself out of some rough scrapes before. Granted this one is a bit different."

Angela shook her head. "Not different. Serious. This is real life. Not just mine but someone else's now. And it's Rafe's life, too."

"Honey, please be calm. Rafe sounds like a very responsible man to me. I've never seen you really fall for a man, that's why I didn't truly worry about you. I don't think you'd ever love someone who didn't love you back, whether he's told you so or not. He'll do the right thing. He'll stand by you and the baby. Think about it. A man who's broken up over having to sell his family's land is the kind of guy who'd make a great father. Everything's going to be great for you two. Uh, three. You've got too much love between you for it not to."

Angela let her tears fall on Julia's shoulder. In her heart she believed Julia was right. She'd never found a man worthy of her love until she'd met Rafe. She wanted to believe they'd been brought together by destiny, even though Matt Leads still insisted upon taking the credit.

She'd felt for a long time that Rafe had a lot of love to give but for some reason he'd kept his feelings bottled up inside.

Julia had always joked that if a man said he loved you

during his passionate lovemaking, it didn't count. He was supposed to declare his love when totally sober, totally clear-headed. Angela had often sensed that Rafe wanted to tell her that he loved her, but those times were only when they were making love.

Angela believed Rafe was a caring and sentimental man just as Julia did. Being with him during Honey Biscuit's illness had showed her his deep empathy for living beings. From his family pride to his sense of needing to belong, he was the only man she ever wanted.

Rafe *would* stand by her. He just had to.

Fourteen

"Angela, I wanted to thank you for the great job you did selling the ranch," Rafe said into her phone recorder. "I know I acted pretty insensitive yesterday. Selfishly, I guess I had a demon or two still in hiding. I missed you last night. I want to see you tonight if that's possible..."

"Rafe?" Angela picked up the phone and asked, breathlessly. "Sorry, I was taking out the garbage and when I came in I heard your voice."

"You know you make me nuts, don't you?" he teased. "I thought I'd go out of mind in that big bed," he paused. "All by myself."

Chewing her bottom lip pensively, she replied, "Do you really mean that?"

"Of course I do. There's another reason, too."

His voice was upbeat, she thought. He must have thought things through and she believed she would like the outcome. "What's that?"

"I got a call this morning from that trainer in Lexington I told you about. He's made me a very good offer on Rising Star and wants me to drive him up tomorrow."

"T—tomorrow?" Angela swallowed hard. *I need more time to think! Time to plan how to tell him about the baby. Slow down, Angela. Think. I shouldn't tell him about the baby tonight. Maybe I should wait until after I go to the doctor. Then, when he's back from Lexington...*

"I want to see you tonight, Angel. I wouldn't blame you for being mad at me for acting so bullheaded last night."

"Mad? No, I'm not mad and I'd love to see you tonight. I have a five o'clock appointment and after that I'll drive out."

"I can't wait. I want to apologize appropriately," he said sensually.

"I'll see you about seven," she replied and after saying goodbye she hung up. Waiting only a moment, Angela picked up the receiver and dialed her gynecologist and booked an appointment for later that morning. The nurse assured her that she'd have the test results back immediately.

Angela was somewhat relieved. She *had* to be sure before she said anything to Rafe.

Rafe greeted Angela with a kiss meant to melt iron. She couldn't help wondering if his kisses would change after she told him the truth.

"You feel so good in my arms," he said with a tone of wonder in his voice. "I don't think I've ever missed anyone as much as I missed you last night."

"You say that as if you find it hard to believe," she replied with a soft, glowing smile.

Nodding solemnly, he said, "I do." He traced the curve

of her jaw with his fingertip. "You've become important to me, in a very short period of time."

Angela could hardly believe her ears. Rafe was trying to tell her that he loved her. This was the moment she'd waited for since the first night they'd met. She'd dreamed of this every night and had believed it would be the most joyous moment of her life. She'd been dead wrong.

Feeling as if she were being strangled by a dark force, anxiety blotted out her happiness. *But will you feel this way when I tell you I've been to see the doctor? Will you ever come to love just me for myself? Even if you decide to marry me, will I ever know if you would have loved me without the baby?*

Angela knew she could keep the truth from him for a few months, or at least until she began to show. Perhaps if she did, then she'd get a better indication of his true feelings for her. But then what would his reaction be? Would he turn away from her because she hadn't told him from the beginning? Would he accuse her of trying to manipulate him once it was too late for an abortion? Would he want her to get rid of the baby or have the baby? Could she ever respect a man who didn't want his own child?

Questioning her own values and integrity, Angela pitted her emotions against the unknown factor of Rafe's reactions and feelings. The outcome was always the same... fear.

Knowledge eliminated fear, she knew. Angela had to know where she stood with Rafe. She couldn't go forward with her life if she didn't.

"Do you love me, Rafe?"

Angela's words hung in the air like a guillotine ready to drop.

Though his mouth was set in a serious firm line, Rafe's eyes sparkled merrily. "I suppose I do."

"Suppose? Either you do or you don't. I know I'm in love with you. Have been for quite some time, now. Since the first time you kissed me, it's been as if I were living someone else's life. I never knew it could be like this…at least not for me."

Taken aback by her straightforward declaration, Rafe pulled her closer. "Didn't anyone ever tell you that patience is a virtue? Hmm?" He nuzzled her neck, then kissed her mouth sweetly. "As it happens I thought a great deal about us last night, lying awake until dawn. I realized how much I look forward to being with you. You've made me laugh again and hope that I could turn my life around. You're a very special lady."

Angela thought she could nearly hear a great big "But, darling" dangling in the air above them like a cartoon balloon. Her stomach knotted. She'd come this far with her probes and tests. She knew she had to go the distance for all their sakes. "This house is full of ghosts, Rafe, and I feel as if I've gotten to know all of them. But there's one you haven't told me about. She stands between us at nearly every corner we turn. I don't even know her name, but I know you must have loved her a great deal for her to still have so much power over you."

Instantly, Rafe's arms fell limply to his sides.

Without saying a word Rafe had given Angela her answer. She knew Rafe might have feelings for her, but he didn't love her in the way she loved him. He was trapped by a life he'd led long before she'd walked in. At that moment, Angela knew what it was like to be jealous. She'd wanted to hold Rafe's heart, but obviously, there was only one woman who'd ever done that. Rafe didn't have room for her, much less their child.

Deeply wounded, Angela stepped back from him. "Maybe I shouldn't be here. Maybe you and I were a mistake right from the beginning. Maybe I should have left that first day when I came here to list the house."

Suddenly, Rafe's eyes flamed with an incredibly intense fire. "Don't ever say that. You're the best thing that's ever happened to me. You just don't know..."

Grabbing her around the waist, Rafe pulled her next to him and kissed her with more passion and intensity than she'd thought possible. Overwhelmed with the ferocity of his kiss, Angela's fears shattered like glass. His lips demanded more emotion, more physical response from her than she'd thought she could give. She succumbed to his demands and let her heart welcome him back. Pressing her body into his, Angela felt transported back to that plane where they'd been one; where love obliterated all fear.

With his lips, tongue and body, Rafe told her all she needed to know about him, about her and their future together. His inability to communicate his feelings was part of his character she'd fallen in love with. She never could have trusted a man who recklessly tossed his emotions around. She would be careful with his heart.

But is it the right time to tell you everything, my love?

Savoring her mouth, Rafe reluctantly ended the kiss. "I had a surprise for you tonight, but you beat me to the draw," he teased, tapping the end of her nose with his forefinger.

"What kind of surprise?" she asked looking up into his beaming face and feeling his love pour into her.

He took her hand. "Come see," he said and pulled her gently into the dining room.

A white Battenburg table cloth was spread out on the floor and set for a formal dinner complete with burning candles in silver candlesticks. "Since this is our last night together for a few days, maybe a week, depending upon how long it takes in Lexington, I thought I'd make tonight extra special."

Spying a single blush rose lying across her plate, Angela remonstrated with herself for her impatience. Rafe clearly had planned a romantic evening. "Remind me to bite my tongue the next time my impatience shows its face."

"I will."

He put his hands on her shoulders and gently nudged her to be seated on the floor while he finished the supper preparations. Lightheartedly, he made a show of each course, pretending to be a French maître d' and speaking in a broken French with a Texas drawl. Angela thought him endearingly charming.

After the meal, they shared the last of a Christmas gift box of chocolates by the fire. Rafe held Angela in his arms as they both contemplated the flames, content with silent intimacy.

Recalling their dinner conversation which Rafe had kept light, yet romantic, Angela sensed she'd done the right thing by deciding to curb her impatience and tell him about the baby once he returned from Lexington. He'd revealed a great deal about himself this evening in all the little things he'd done.

Kissing the top of Angela's head, Rafe said, "Give me some time, Angela. One of the things you should know about me is that I'm quite old-fashioned. I believe a man should be able to put his honor on the line when he finally finds the woman he's been searching for. A man's responsibility to the woman he loves should be a real commitment on his part. He's got to be able to take care of her." He squeezed her shoulders as he continued. "I don't make commitments lightly, Angela."

"Nor do I," she whispered thinking about their baby.

"It's just that I want everything to be right for us. I have tremendous financial entanglements that I want to clear away before I can do anything else. If I seem hesitant about us...I don't mean to be," he said, frustratedly running his hand through his hair. "I'm not saying this correctly," he sighed.

Angela tilted her face up to him. "I understand what you're trying to say and it's all right, Rafe," she said.

"Are you sure?"

"Yes."

His eyes were deep sapphire blue as he gazed at her. "I know what you want and I intend to be the man to give it all to you. I just need some time."

Kissing his chin, Angela nodded.

"Right now I want to take you up to bed and make love with you. I need to be inside you, Angela." He kissed her ravenously. "I need you badly."

Awakening the next morning, Angela stretched like a cat and nearly purred, she was so happy. She rolled over to find Rafe still sound asleep though it was past six and he usually would have been up for an hour to feed the horses.

Their lovemaking last night had never been more hauntingly divine. She found it incredible that Rafe continued to reach parts of her soul she hadn't known existed. He knew her better than she knew herself.

She wondered how long she would have gone through life thinking, like so many people, that love was something that could be developed by two well-intentioned people with mutual interests. Her friends had introduced her to dozens of men who they thought would be "perfect" for her. But nothing like this ever happened to her.

Love was an inexplicable magic, Angela decided. But destiny was love's magician.

Rolling onto his side, Rafe opened his eyes and smiled. "Good morning, sunshine."

"Good morning," she replied happily and kissed him. "We overslept."

Rafe's stomach growled as he pulled her to him for another kiss. "I don't care. You were delicious last night, but now I'm starved. I'll volunteer to fix breakfast," he said getting out of bed and putting on his jeans.

Angela rose slowly feeling oddly light-headed. She stuck her arms into Rafe's old robe.

"What do you feel like?" he asked breezily more to himself than to her as he buttoned his shirt. "Eggs? Grits? Some toast and bacon maybe. Lots of coffee! Yeah," he whistled merrily to himself as he kissed her cheek quickly. "By the time you're dressed, I'll have a good old-fashioned country breakfast waiting." He left the room still mumbling his options aloud. "Biscuits and gravy. Honey..."

Envisioning bacon frying in a skillet and raw eggs sizzling in the fat, Angela's eyes flew open. She could almost feel herself turning a bilious green. Her stomach lurched. She grabbed the edges of the robe and rushed to the bathroom where she vomited.

All Rafe's talk about food had made her sick, she thought as she heaved again. Turning on the water faucet she ran the water over her hand and then pressed her cold fingers to her forehead.

In seconds, she threw up again. This had nothing to do with Rafe's menu. It was as if the baby was angry with her for not telling Rafe the truth. Mentally assuring herself she would address the situation when Rafe was back from his trip, she was finally able to rise from the commode and slowly get dressed.

In twenty minutes Angela was dressed for work. Knowing she needed to run by her townhouse, check on Rebel and her messages before going into the office, she told Rafe she didn't have time for a large breakfast.

"Honestly, dry toast is fine."

"It's not enough. Besides, I have to leave here in a couple hours myself. I won't see you for nearly a week," he pleaded.

"All right," she smiled and sat at the table while Rafe placed two eggs, bacon and fresh biscuits loaded with butter and honey in front of her. She sipped the hot coffee. In her condition it tasted like acid.

Slamming her hand over her mouth, she bolted out of the chair. She knew she'd never make it to the guest bath. She nearly flew to the kitchen sink. She heaved. Her stomach lurched and she heaved again, but nothing remained inside her but water.

"Angela? Are you all right?" Rafe was at her side in seconds.

She shook her head but didn't dare move. She might heave again.

"Was it the fish from last night? Maybe I didn't grill it long enough?"

"No, it was fine." She felt her muscles clench and her back arch as a new wave of dry heaves overtook her. Finally, she said, "I'm all right. Really."

"You're white as a sheet. Maybe it's the flu. I could call the doctor…" Rafe started toward the wall phone.

"I've already seen the doctor and he's seen me," she said. "Seen us, I mean." Her insides felt hollow, but somehow she'd found the courage to tell him.

Stopping dead in his tracks, Rafe's back was ramrod stiff. "Us?"

Angela's mouth was dry, but still she managed to swallow hard. "The doctor told me I'm pregnant, Rafe," she said.

Keeping his back to her he asked, "And you weren't going to tell me about it?"

"When you got back. I was going to tell you then."

"Why then? That's a week from now," his voice was caustic and bitter-sounding.

"I know how important it is for you to feel financially grounded."

"Is that right?"

She hated talking to his back like this. She hated not seeing his eyes. He held his body still and hard like stone. "You said as much last night."

"Maybe you felt you needed this week to prepare."

Thinking the air between them had turned to ice, Angela stumbled over her words. "I wanted to say it the right way...."

Slowly, he turned toward her. His clenched jaw was as intractable as his steel gray eyes. "How can there be a right way and a wrong way? It either is or it isn't. Maybe you needed some time to figure out how you were going to tell me that your baby isn't mine."

Too stunned to answer, Angela could only stare at him.

"Well," he huffed angrily. "Is it mine?"

Is it mine? The words screamed across Angela's mind like banshees. She felt her blood turn to ice and her heart stand still. In her most bizarre imaginings, Angela had never prepared herself for this response. Never had she thought betrayal could cut so deep.

Looking into his brittle eyes she could see he believed it was possible she had lied to him about loving him. That she'd used him for some twisted personal reasons. She didn't need to hear another word from him. She'd deluded herself with Rafe Whitten for the last time.

He was nothing like the kind of man her great-grandfather had been. It was just as Julia and Ilsa had warned, she'd invented a fantasy hero out of Rafe and now she would pay the price. Because she'd let the illusion go too far, she'd live with the consequences for the rest of her life.

She could defend herself by flinging the truth at him but it would roll off him. She'd already wasted months of her own precious life caught in Rafe's sensuous web. He'd wanted time. Well, she was going to give him plenty of it.

From this moment on, she'd never see him again. Never believe in him or in her own judgment again. She was a fool. A pregnant fool.

"The baby is mine, Rafe."

Quickly, she grabbed her purse from the kitchen counter and left the house.

Angela didn't look back.

Fifteen

"Is it mine?"

The sound of his own voice caused Rafe's world to explode around him. Stunned by a slicing familiar pain, Rafe's mind blocked out the present as if Angela had never existed. He found himself travelling through time to a place in the past he'd vowed never to revisit. It was a time when he thought he'd been in love. It was Cheryl's time.

Before Cheryl, Rafe hadn't the slightest idea what it was like to be conned by a woman. Even the girls he'd dated in high school were kind, sweet and from good families. Though they all explored their approaching sexuality and coming-of-age together, none of his friends, boys or girls, ever toppled the barriers of the Southern moral code of conduct they believed was the essence of being an adult.

Rafe's experiences had been that for the most part,

women were as trustworthy as himself. What he hadn't factored into his calculations was the life-changing cata- lyst of his million-dollar company. Rafe had catapulted himself into unexplored territory where his character was less important than his financial statement. In this barren universe, he was no longer the creator, the inventor of new ideas. He was the target.

When Rafe first met Cheryl, he thought she was the most sensuous, long-legged blond beauty he'd ever known. She seemed to anticipate his every need. If he was tired, she proposed a quiet dinner at home where she immediately propped his head on the softest pillow in her apartment. He only had to lick his dry lips and she handed him an icy drink. When his business calls came in, she turned down the stereo and exited the room. When he was in a romantic mood, she knew all the scene-setting props to use.

He didn't realize it at the time, but Cheryl made his life easy. She took care of their social life, lining up dinner reservations, ordering the best chardonnays to be chilled and waiting for them at their table. She arranged for his cleaning to be picked up and delivered to his penthouse so that when he found he had to dash out of town for a business meeting, packing was a breeze.

Cheryl moved into his life, his apartment and even some aspects of his business without his realizing her presence. Until it was too late.

Rafe's business had rocketed to the top. It seemed to him and just about everyone around him that nothing could or would stop him. He didn't have time to think about Cheryl's motivations, nor was there any reason to. She *acted* as if he was the most important person in her life. She called him "darling" and "her man." She made him feel sexy, wanted, needed…and bigger than life.

Somehow, Cheryl had known precisely how to massage and manipulate his ego without giving herself away.

Lying awake in the still night on the ranch was the only time when life slowed down enough for Rafe to ponder his relationship with Cheryl. At those times he could almost feel a nagging, tickling feeling in the center of his solar plexus, telling him that something wasn't quite right. He couldn't help wondering why, even after he'd spent an evening with Cheryl, he always felt alone when he returned home. He'd listened to enough love songs in his life to know that somewhere a songwriter knew something he didn't know. According to them, Rafe should be feeling complete, not empty. He should be seeing his children in Cheryl's eyes, but he didn't. He should be planning to spend his old age with her, but he didn't think she'd appreciate the notion. Cheryl was energetic and filled his life with fun. She often said she'd had a hard childhood. Now she wanted to "live." And live they did. Didn't they?

Cheryl's kisses were sexual and passionate, but since he'd never been in love before, he guessed that perhaps he was asking too much of love when he thought there should be something "more."

If only he could describe to himself what that something more was, maybe everything might have turned out differently.

Rafe remembered a particularly hot summer day when he'd gone to the ranch. Talking to his ranch hands about some repairs that needed to be made, Rafe hadn't realized Cheryl had arrived and was standing behind him. Something about her explanation for being there had not settled right with him. She insisted on making lemonade for everyone rather than going back to Houston as he requested.

She took up over two hours of his time with unnecessary small talk, which he felt they could have shared at dinner that night. As it was, Rafe had to push their dinner reservations at Café Annie back to nine o'clock. Finally, frustrated at having to keep shuffling his plans, he shooed Cheryl away. She made him promise to call her from his cellular phone when he was thirty minutes from the city. She told him she wanted to do some last-minute shopping. Then she laughed and skipped down the steps to the new white Jaguar convertible he'd leased for her. He watched her drive away, her blond hair flowing in the hot sparkling sun.

Waving to her, it was the first time Rafe knew that the tickle in his gut was because he didn't trust Cheryl.

Rafe finished his work at the ranch and on his way back into town he called his penthouse several times but Cheryl never picked up. He could only guess she was still out shopping. She was fanatical about her appearance when they went to the finer restaurants, where stringers for the media parked themselves hoping to snag a juicy piece of gossip for the columns.

Because Rafe's business was going so well, he'd given Cheryl an open account at Tootsie's and Ester Wolfe's. Nothing pleased Rafe more than to see her eyes light up when he approved of the ensemble she'd carefully put together. He didn't complain about the money she spent, even though several times he'd raised his eyebrows over the price tags.

Money didn't matter much to Rafe since he'd always had enough to eat and a place to sleep. He'd never been a greedy person and even considered himself a generous person. Rafe only wanted large amounts of money in order to stay a "player" in the entrepreneurial game. Though he'd worked hard to get his company up and rolling, he'd never been a possessive kind of person. He enjoyed seeing his ideas become reality.

Paul Thomas, Rafe's business partner and buddy since their college days at the University of Texas, fretted over the expenses more than Rafe ever did. Often, Rafe kidded Paul that he was going to be a young man with a heart attack if he didn't learn that business was nothing but a game.

Having majored in accounting, Paul was the typical shy fellow chained to his computer, calculator and ledger sheets. He had no friends in Houston other than Rafe. His family lived in Wichita Falls, where his father still worked as an executive for a popular pizza chain. Though Paul was tall, slender and good-looking in a studious way, he never seemed to date anyone seriously. He was content to spend his weekends playing on the computer either at the office or at his apartment near the Galleria. Even when Rafe and Cheryl invited him to dinner with them or to a baseball game, Paul always declined, claiming he "had work to do."

After working with Paul for nearly eighteen months, Rafe realized Paul was neither as quick-minded nor as organized as he was himself. Paul plodded through his work, whereas Rafe was already a dozen steps ahead.

Punching out his office number, Rafe hoped to catch Paul before he left for the day. When Verna, the secretary, answered she told him that Paul had left a couple of hours ago, saying he'd have his cellular phone on in case she or Rafe needed him.

Rafe dialed Paul's cellular number and found it was turned off. He left a message telling Paul he would see him in the morning and that he was just checking in.

Fifteen minutes from his penthouse just outside the

Loop, Rafe called his home number. There was still no answer. It was after five, which meant that Cheryl was no doubt caught in traffic somewhere on Post Oak.

Rafe got home, showered, shaved and dressed in his best designer pinstripe suit and crocodile shoes. He opened a bottle of chardonnay and placed a CD on the player while waiting for Cheryl.

At six-thirty Cheryl let herself in with the key he'd given her several months ago.

"Rafe! What are you doing here?"

"I live here," he replied.

Flustered and a bit anxious as she glanced around the room, Cheryl tried to be playful. "I didn't expect you till seven when I would have been dressed."

"I tried to call you but your cellular phone was turned off," he said, noticing suddenly that she wasn't playful in the least. She was jumpy and quite anxious about something.

"I didn't turn it off. Omigosh! I'll bet I forgot to charge the battery last night." She walked over to an antique cane chair she'd told him she thought was ugly and picked up the jacket he intended to wear that evening. She reached in the pocket where he always kept his flip phone. "Since your phone is no doubt working, I can use your battery."

"Why not just recharge yours?" he asked cautiously, as he rose and slowly walked toward her. *Something isn't right...I can feel it.* "There's something bothering you," he said seriously.

Taking a deep breath, she turned away from him and walked over to the wall of glass that overlooked the city. It was hours until nightfall and the swathe of wispy clouds across the horizon promised another incredibly brilliant sunset. "I'm pregnant, Rafe," she said in a voice laden with lament.

"You're what?" he gasped.

"Pregnant. Nearly three months, the doctor said. Too late to have an abortion, he said, though I think I can find someone who'll do it for me."

The words slammed into Rafe's brain like a derailed train. His intuition had been warning him about her "secret," and erroneously he'd thought she was distrustful rather than realizing she just might be afraid to tell him the truth. Rafe felt his fears shatter instantly. He wanted to simultaneously laugh and cry at his own silliness. But abortion? She was talking about *their* baby. He had to let her know how he felt about such things.

Rafe was across the room in a millisecond. "Now you listen to me," he said taking her shoulders in his hands. "You'll do nothing of the kind. I think this is wonderful news! I'm not afraid of being a father. In fact, I relish the idea. There's nothing I want more than to raise a couple of kids..."

"A couple?"

"Okay, if you want more, we'll have them. I hated being the only child. I like the idea of a big family. This is wonderful!" he said, giving her a hug. "Please don't ever think I'd want you to...get rid of my baby."

"It's not your baby."

It was like being shot with a gun. Rafe felt the pain before he heard the sound. His heart stopped. His mind spun out of control. Inhaling and exhaling at the same time caused him to feel as if the wind had been knocked out of him. He must have heard her wrong, he decided. The mother of his child could never be this cruel. She would never intentionally hurt him, would she? This was a mistake, a misunderstanding on his part.

Finally, he drew in enough air to say, "You're kidding."

Cheryl simply shook her head with an odd smile that turned into a revelation of her soul. She seemed almost relieved to have the truth come out.

Rafe unleashed his emotions. "This is insane. Of course it's mine."

"How can you be so naive, Rafe?"

He stared disbelievingly at her. "Naive? What the hell are you talking about?"

Cheryl smirked at him but remained silent. Had he been a vengeful man he might have wanted to strike her.

He'd always prided himself on self-control. "For the last time, tell me the truth."

"The baby isn't yours."

"Then who..." Rafe lost his voice.

"It doesn't matter," she whispered, dropping her head so as not to look at him.

"It sure as hell matters to me!"

"Why? Because it hurts your male ego to know I was doing someone else while I was doing you? You may think you're sexy and virile and all that macho stuff, but I need a whole lot more than you put out. I tried to tell you what I needed, but you were always too busy, or on your way to another meeting."

She doesn't know me in the least, he thought, listening to her description of the kind of man even he despised. How ironic it was that she hadn't known his true character any more than he'd known hers. "I was thinking about our future," he replied calmly.

"Bull! You men all say that but what's really going on is that you get off making your deals. No wonder there's nothing left for me but a few kisses and holding hands over dinner. I need more, Rafe. A lot more!"

Suddenly, Cheryl whirled around and headed for the door. Her face was crimson with anger though she tried to calm herself by breathing deeply. She stopped at the door and, with a measure of calm, she said, "Look, I didn't think things would go this far. I thought we were having fun. Some kicks. Great sex. I liked that the best. But this talk of yours about babies and families... The next thing I know is you'll be wanting me to go live in that rat trap out in Waller!"

"It's my family's home. It means a great deal to me."

"It means nothing to me." She pulled her key out of her purse and placed it on the console near the door. Grasping the doorknob she said, "One thing I want to get straight between us, Rafe, I'll do a lot of things for a man, but I won't have anybody's brat!"

She'd finally pushed him to the breaking point. He grabbed her arm. "Fine. Since it's not mine I don't give a damn. But you're not leaving here until you tell me whose baby it is...if you know."

Snarling at him, she said, "You bet I know. Paul Thomas."

Stumbling backward, Rafe reached for the wall to steady himself. The impact of Cheryl's words split through his world like an earthquake. He'd prepared himself to hear the name of a faceless stranger or even one of Cheryl's old boyfriends, but never had he thought it would be his best friend.

Rafe went to the mirrored bar and took a bottle of Scotch off the glass shelf and poured himself a deep drink. He dialed Paul's home number but there was no answer. He dialed his partner's cellular number and heard a recording stating the number was no longer in service. Not believing his ears, he called the phone company. The operator assured him the cellular number had been disconnected.

Shivering as if someone had walked over his grave, Rafe had a feeling he was about to find out just how deeply he'd been betrayed by both his partner and his girlfriend.

Leaving the Scotch on the bar, Rafe raced to the elevator.

By the time Rafe reached the corporate offices of Eagle Tech, night was falling fast. He unlocked the doors, greeted the night cleaning crew and rushed to Paul's office.

The room was stripped of Paul's personal things, his plants and plastic cartoon cat collection.

A quick investigation revealed that Paul had taken all the company records, loaded them onto floppy disks and then deleted everything from the computer's hard drive. Rafe knew it would take weeks, possibly months to recreate his work.

Never having experienced the kind of rage he felt now, he vowed he would not sleep or eat until he avenged himself against his betrayers. For Rafe, there was only one way to get revenge. He had to make Eagle Tech a success no matter what it took.

Looking like a black hole in space, the empty computer screen stared back at Rafe. This was only the beginning, but Rafe knew he was walking into hell.

The sound of spinning tires on gravel shook Rafe out of his reverie and back to the present. Angela was leaving him.

"Is it mine?"

Rafe was alone with the echoing memory of his own

words. Dazed and confused, Rafe glanced around the room for Angela. *She wouldn't leave me, too. Would she?*

Then he heard a car drive off.

"Angela?" He raced to the front door and opened it. "Angela!"

Please don't go, Angela. You don't understand. I thought you were someone else.

Suddenly, Rafe's thought hit him between the eyes. "I thought you were like *her*. What a fool I've been!"

Angela and Cheryl were as alike as negative is to positive. Angela was everything he'd ever wanted in a woman, but hadn't found. She was sweet and kind like his mother, yet intelligent, hardworking and fiercely independent, just like himself. Angela was a blend of his ideals and his reality.

He'd meant what he'd said to Cheryl when he thought he was going to be a father. Rafe wanted children and a loving relationship with a woman who felt the same as he. In his life, he'd gone to the summit of success and found the whole thing a crock without the right woman to share it with. He wanted the same kind of life his parents had lived. He wanted to know what it was like to hold his own child on the day of its birth. Deep inside himself he knew he possessed an ability to care for his children the way he'd been cared for. He had dreamed of sharing his every moment with a wife who would love him enough to give him a child. But for such a very long time he'd kept all his needs locked in so tightly it was a wonder Angela had stayed with him as long as she had.

For the first time he recognized that ache deep inside for what it was. His need to love had been killed by fears of his own creation. When he thought of the nights he'd pretended he was doing well on his own and how he'd perpetuated his "lie" by surrounding himself with people, he laughed at the absurdity of it all.

Ráking his hand through his hair, wondering what to do, he spied the phone. He dialed Angela's car phone but it was busy. He hit the Redial button. Still busy.

What had he been thinking? Whenever he'd made love with Angela he'd felt as if his world had been born again but he'd been so blinded by the pain of Cheryl's betrayal that he couldn't see Angela for the giving, loving person she was.

Hanging up the phone, he grabbed his riding boots which were standing by the front door and shoved his feet inside, nearly toppling over in his haste. He raced outside and headed toward the corral where Rising Star lifted his head at the sound of his master's voice.

Rafe threw open the gate and rushed into the horse barn to gather a horse blanket and saddle. "We can still catch her, boy," he said to the horse as he placed the bit in Rising Star's mouth and then pulled the cinches tight. "She can't outrun us."

The horse whinnied and neighed as if he knew exactly what Rafe meant. Sticking his booted foot in the stirrup, Rafe swung his right leg over the horse's flanks and spurred the horse to a gallop with his knees.

Just as he was out of the gate, Rafe heard the ear splitting sound of the horse barn phone ringing.

"Angela!" Rafe couldn't get unseated fast enough. "She's calling from her car. Thank God!" *She must have been trying to call me when I was dialing her number.* He ran into the barn and picked up the phone. "Hello! Angela? Thank God…"

"Rafe?" A man's voice said. "We must have a bad connection. Is this Rafe Whitten?"

"Yes, it is," Rafe replied feeling the expectant air in

his lungs ignite, burn and turn to cinders as his hope died. He recognized the raspy voice of Fred MacIvers, the horse trainer from Lexington who had agreed to buy Rising Star. "What can I do for you, Fred?"

"I hadn't heard from you. I was hoping you'd be on the road by now."

On the road. Angela is on the road and I must get to her. I don't have much time. I can still make it. "Sorry, but I have to go, Fred. I'll call you in a bit."

Leaving the receiver dangling from the wall, Rafe shot out of the barn, took a running leap over Rising Star's flanks and landed in the saddle. "Let's go, boy!" Rafe smacked Rising Star's back with his hand and the horse took off at a full gallop.

Leaning over Rising Star's neck to gain speed, Rafe whispered prayers to himself. *Please let me catch her. Please, God.*

Clumps of Rising Star's windswept mane flew in Rafe's eyes, obscuring his vision, but within moments he saw the roostertail of gravel spinning out from beneath Angela's tires. She was driving recklessly fast over the treacherously rutted road.

Couldn't she see where she was going? he thought as the car swerved perilously close to the deep gully on the side of the road. Suddenly, the car righted itself as Angela slowed down and worked her way around the eroding pits in the road.

Then Rafe saw her wipe her eyes with the palm of her hand. She was crying. With her eyes filled with tears it was a wonder she'd made it this far.

Rafe felt the pit of his stomach yawn, freeing his pent-up emotions. His nerves jangled and fear thundered through his head as her car careened recklessly around a sharp bend.

Be careful, darling.

"Angela! Stop!" he yelled but he could tell she hadn't so much as glanced at the rearview mirror. He wondered if she had seen him. Would she stop? Would she wait for him? Would she listen to him if she did?

"C'mon, boy, I know you can do it. Just a little farther."

Man and horse raced through the thickening pine trees. Rafe ducked to avoid low-hanging poisonous vines, then gripped the saddle horn as he leaned out of the saddle to avoid limb after limb. The scent of Southern pine and rotted leaves wet with old rain filled Rafe's nostrils reminding him of the times he'd shared with Angela here on his ranch. He remembered how he'd held her thinking the feeling was *too* familiar, too comfortable to trust. She'd looked in his eyes offering her soul to him and he'd taken it without giving back any of his. The sweet haunting memory of her completed the last thread of the fabric that could have been their life together.

Rising Star jumped a narrow creek, dodged a rabbit hole and turned the bend as he raced alongside the white fence separating Whitten land from the public road.

Angela's car drew closer as she was forced to work around ruts and potholes. However, Rafe knew that if he didn't catch her attention soon, she'd reach the newly graveled section of road. Then she'd hit the highway where Rising Star was no match for her car.

"Angela!" Rafe yelled again. He waved his arm and whistled.

Watching her as she glanced in the rearview mirror then instantly hit the brake, Rafe thought he'd never seen a more beautiful sight than her illuminated red brake lights. Only his smile could shine any brighter.

Thank God...

Rafe kept racing toward Angela, convinced she was about to pull to a stop. Disbelieving, he watched as she clearly turned to watch him approach, then she lowered her head, looked back at the road ahead of her and hit the gas.

Tires spun, gravel flew, dust rose in a column around the car rendering it invisible to Rafe long enough for Angela to make her getaway.

By the time Rafe reached the end of his property, Angela had vanished into the distance. In seconds she would be on Highway 290.

Reining Rising Star to a halt, Rafe slid off his horse. Rider and mount were both panting with exhaustion. He walked to the fence, and angrily pounded his fist on the top rail. Rafe felt defeated—would he never have the chance to convince Angela he'd been a fool?

He shoved his hands in his jeans pockets. *A fool... bankrupt and soon to be homeless.*

He kicked a rock. "*That* ought to really convince her! No wonder she kept on driving. Some prize I turned out to be."

Sixteen

Angela turned off the ringer on all the extension phones and unplugged the phone recorder. She didn't want to hear from Rafe, nor did she want interference from Julia or Ilsa. She desperately needed time to think.

"Is it mine?" Rafe's accusatory question reverberated in her head.

Not once had Angela ever considered the idea that Rafe did not trust her. Unthinkable as the idea was to her, he'd proved in those three words that he'd never considered himself to be in love with her. What she'd been feeling as a spiritual connection between them had been illusion on her part. Once she'd discovered his true feelings about her character, there was no point in discussing his involvement in her life or her baby's life. Angela needed to come to grips with the reality that she and her baby were about to face life without Rafe.

Rushing over her like a tumultuous hurricane sea, sorrow drowned her anger and sadness filled her heart. The pain of losing Rafe went so deep that Angela didn't cry. She stared blankly out the window at a winter robin perched on a barren tree limb. Numbly, she wondered what it would be like to fly away from all her problems. Would she feel free? Or would she feel doubly burdened with guilt?

Her answers evolved slowly, but clearly in her head. She'd been without a family for much too long. She wasn't a kid anymore and didn't want a life filled with mindless activities just to kill time. She wanted a real life, she'd wanted a complete family, but perhaps for some women, a husband wasn't the answer. She'd meant it when she told Rafe the baby was hers. She didn't need Rafe to support her financially. Frankly, she was doing a whole lot better than he was at the moment. She could turn the spare bedroom into a nursery in less than a month. There were plenty of kind and responsible nannies in Houston. She'd sold houses to many clients who'd often mentioned their excellent nannies.

Evaluating her past year with Randy had shown Angela that she'd allowed her sales to slip because she'd been bored. She didn't respect Randy or his policies any longer. Perhaps she'd been looking for an excuse to muster the courage to strike out on her own. She was smart enough, she'd been in the real estate business long enough to know that all she needed was courage.

Placing her hands over her abdomen, Angela smiled. Her baby was giving her the strength to look at a great many options.

She could do anything she wanted. No one was stopping her from learning more, getting more education, stretching her intellect and creativity to her limits. Now that the baby had given her a new sense of purpose, she saw a myriad of new goals she wanted to accomplish.

With a new vision of her future, Angela realized she didn't have time for bitterness toward Rafe nor would she waste energy criticizing herself for falling in love with the wrong man. She'd given Rafe her heart. She'd been honest with her feelings. The fact that he didn't reciprocate was neither right or wrong. It simply didn't work out.

Holding grudges was a waste of time for her. That kind of mind set would do nothing but harm her baby and herself as well. She didn't want her child to grow up thinking that his or her father was anything less than perfect.

Angela had lived a love-filled idyll with Rafe Whitten. It was a time she'd never forget. For her, it had been perfect, but it was over. Angela's only choice was to move forward.

Last-minute details of closing the house, packing feed, hay and Rising Star's favorite brushes along with his own clothes were clouded by Rafe's thoughts about Angela. He knew he should have been on the road already in order to make tomorrow's early-morning appointment with Fred MacIvers in Lexington. He'd have to drive all night as it was, but he couldn't help dialing Angela's number repeatedly.

Leaving a half-dozen messages at work for her to call him on his cellular phone, in frustration, Rafe finally called the phone company.

"There's something wrong with the number I'm dialing. I wonder if you could check it out for me."

"Yes, sir. One moment," the service representative said. After a long moment she came back on the line. "I'm sorry, sir. That line has been disconnected."

"Disconnected?"

"Yes, sir, at the subscriber's request."

"Thanks." Rafe knew that for the time being, until he returned from Lexington, he'd have little chance of finding Angela to talk to her.

After two hours on the road, Rafe turned off his cellular phone. Admitting to himself that Angela was right not to contact him was a difficult realization, but it was the truth. How was he going to even start his apology? *Sorry, I thought I was over Cheryl, but obviously I wasn't, but I am now? The pain she inflicted was such a part of me that I didn't appreciate someone wonderful?*

He raked his hair with his hand. God, just how big a jerk can I be?

"Pretty damn big, Rafe," he mumbled to himself as he passed a vintage Cadillac driven by an elderly man wearing a straw hat.

The man smiled and waved to Rafe as if he'd known him for years. Rafe lifted his arm, but didn't smile back.

How odd. My grandfather used to drive a car like that. I remember seeing photographs of it. Mother used to say it was the prettiest car she'd ever seen.

Past family memories filled Rafe's mind. He saw himself lying on a red-and-white checked tablecloth under a grove of trees, his father looming over him with a happy smile telling two-year-old Rafe how proud he was of his son. Giggling, Rafe had thrown his arms around his father's neck and told him how much he loved him.

He remembered his mother cutting an apple pie and serving their picnic lunch. Though only a toddler, Rafe's mind had absorbed every detail of the moment. He could recall the spicy aftershave his father wore when he bent his head, placed his mouth against Rafe's bare belly and made funny bubbling noises that tickled and made Rafe laugh even more.

"Always remember, Rafe, there's nothing more important in this world than family," Rafe's father had once told him when Rafe was about eight, while they were flying kites together on a windy early March afternoon. "This has been a spectacular year for us on the ranch. Your mother sure is enjoying that new refrigerator and sewing machine I bought her. But you know, son, my father always told me that his greatest accomplishment was having me as a son."

Rafe had looked up at his father with awe. "Did you do anything special, Dad?"

"Nope. Just loved him back," he said never taking his eyes from the kite.

"I think you're the best father in the whole world."

Rubbing Rafe's shock of thick hair with his hand, his father said, "You've been a joy to me since the day you were born, Rafe. I'm proud of the way you conduct yourself with your friends. I've noticed how they look to you for advice and such. That's quite an accomplishment at your age."

"Aw, they only do that 'cuz they don't want me to call them stupid when they do stupid stuff."

His father chuckled. "That's what I mean. Wisdom usually comes with age or experience or both. You were born with a large dose. Don't ever lose that, son. It'll see you through some rough spots."

"What kind of spots?" Rafe asked.

"Troubled times. Painful times. Everyone has them from time to time." He hugged his son's shoulders. "But you'll be fine. You know what's important in life."

Feeling as though his father was sitting in the truck talking to him, Rafe glanced twice at the empty seat next to him to make sure he wasn't hallucinating.

You know what's important in life.

Angela. She was his life. When they'd first met, Rafe felt as if he'd been struck by a thunderbolt. Looking into her eyes during their first dance at the Post Oak Ranch, her caring and loving ways had reached out to him and touched him even then. Their first kiss had unnerved him enough to frighten the bejesus out of him. He'd actually walked away from her pretending not to feel his own emotions. Angela had broken through the icy prison he'd erected around his heart.

But Matt had seen through his charade.

Being without her now was torturous. Knowing she didn't want any part of him, not even communication, hurt him deeply.

He supposed he deserved her anger in a way. It was payback for the way he'd treated her at the beginning of their affair. Rafe remembered purposefully deciding that all he wanted from Angela was sex. He'd never lusted for a woman the way he had Angela. No matter how many times he'd kissed her, held her, entered her, it was never enough. Truthfully, making love with Angela was as close to an addiction as he ever wanted to get. If not for her work schedule he doubted he would ever have let her out of bed. He recalled racking his brain trying to understand what had come over him.

Then he realized he'd wanted *more* from Angela than just sex. He'd wanted to probe her psyche, then her heart. Even that wasn't enough. Rafe was obsessed with possessing Angela's soul. He'd discovered what it was like to be so completely part of another person that he'd lost every trace of his own identity. He loved her that completely.

There was no doubt in his mind that he and Angela had created a child at the moment he'd surrendered his ego to hers and placed her heart, her needs, before his own. He'd meant it when he'd said she was his angel. She'd shown him paradise.

"Paradise is lost now, buddy," Rafe said sardonically to himself as he reached for the cellular and turned it back on. "And you have no one to blame but yourself."

He punched out Angela's work number. It was picked up by Angela's friend Ilsa.

"Hi, Ilsa. This is Rafe Whitten. I really need to talk with Angela. Is she there?"

Ilsa's cheery voice instantly turned cold. "She's here, Rafe, but she specifically requested that I tell you she's not taking your calls."

Anxiety dried Rafe's mouth. "Ilsa, please. She doesn't understand."

"Wrong," Ilsa replied in whispered tones. "She's got a real clear-cut picture, believe me."

Rafe could nearly hear the unspoken derogatory names that Ilsa would have called him had she not been at work. "I need to explain some things to her. Very important things that happened a long time ago. They have nothing to do with her, but I've let my past come between us. I…"

Ilsa broke in. "Look, you wanna leave a message for her? I'll write it down. That's my job. You're a client and I could get the ax if I didn't."

"You'd give her my message?" Rafe asked suddenly brightening.

"I don't want to, but I figure a…creep like you would get me in trouble with my boss if I didn't. I wouldn't put anything past you."

Smiling, Rafe replied, "Thank God you're so conscientious about your job, Ilsa. Tell Angela I'm driving straight through. I was planning to stay in Lexington for a few days, but the minute I conclude my business, I'll drive straight back. I need to talk to her. Tell her that I love her. Tell her that I'm very, very happy about..." Suddenly, he stopped himself as he realized that Ilsa might not know about their baby. "About everything. Tell her I was a jerk and that I'm very sorry she's upset with me. I'll make everything right when I get back to Houston."

He paused. "Do you have all that?"

"I've got it. Anything else?"

"Yeah, tell her to plug her phone back in. I'd like to talk to her tonight before she goes to sleep."

"Okay," Ilsa replied and hung up.

Peeling the memo sheet from the message pad, Ilsa walked into Angela's office. "Do you want me to take any calls from Rafe?"

"No," Angela said not lifting her eyes from the title work she was proofing for Rafe's ranch.

"No messages if he gives me any?"

"No." She looked up at Ilsa as she realized what Ilsa was saying. "He called?"

"Yeah." Ilsa held out the message. "Do you want to see this?"

"Sure." Angela took the note glanced at it briefly to get the gist of the meaning, then tore up the paper and put the pieces in the wastebasket.

"Are you okay?" Ilsa asked.

Smiling confidently, Angela answered, "I've never been better."

Seventeen

Upon his return from Lexington, Rafe found messages from two horse-racing owners wanting to purchase Honey Biscuit. After listening to several messages from creditors Rafe heard Angela's voice.

"Rafe, I've received word from the title company that your closing is set for two weeks from Thursday at ten in the morning. All the paperwork seems to be in order. If you have any problem with this day or time, please call Ilsa at our office so that we can make other arrangements."

Angela's voice was professional and calm, and he could not detect a trace of bitterness. However, neither could he hear the sound of soft caring he remembered so well.

Grabbing the kitchen wall phone, Rafe punched out Angela's phone number at home. It was a futile effort, he knew, since he'd tried to call her from Lexington and from every pay phone in Kentucky, Arkansas and Texas when his cellular was incapable of picking up a signal. She'd never answered, but at least she'd plugged the phone back in and he'd been able to leave a message. By the end of the trip, he'd called nearly a dozen times just to hear the sound of her voice on the recorder.

He knew today would be no different.

The phone was ringing as Angela was on her way out the door. Without thinking, she put down her briefcase and answered it.

"Angela?" Rafe sounded as if he couldn't believe his good luck. "You must not be mad at me anymore if you're not screening your calls."

She paused for a long moment, stunned at how much his voice affected her. Looking down at her hands she was surprised to find them shaking. "I was just leaving for a showing." She reminded herself that she was strong now. She didn't need him for anything.

But do I want him? What a stupid question to ask herself. Of course she wanted him, but on her terms. He'd made it all too clear that would never be possible.

"I want to see you today. After your showing."

"I can't."

"Can't or won't?" he asked.

"Both. I'll save you the asking. I don't want to see you today or tomorrow. We have nothing to discuss. I'm fine, Rafe. You're fine. Your ranch is selling sooner than we'd expected. Everything in your life is in order. So is mine." She inhaled deeply, remembering that courage was more easily found when she remained calm.

"Are you nuts? Nothing is 'in order.' Everything is about as messed up as it can be and I take full blame for it."

"Rafe, I have to go," she said starting to hang up the phone.

"You will see me, Angela! Damn, don't hang this phone up!"

Angela placed the receiver on the hook, petted Rebel then checked her purse for her keys. With briefcase in hand, she left the house.

Stalking a woman was the last thing Rafe ever thought he'd do, but if he had to resort to it to win Angela back, he'd do it.

After spending the late afternoon sitting in his truck in a parking lot across the street from Angela's realty office, he followed her to a small restaurant on Woodway where she sat with Julia and Ilsa having drinks by a window side table. He noticed that she ordered what appeared to be a soft drink while the others had wine. Watching while Julia, with a dour face, listened attentively to Angela, Rafe realized that Angela's expression was just as animated as it had ever been. She was not upset in the least about their breakup and apparently *she* was going through none of the pain he'd been feeling.

Whatever it was they were discussing, Rafe could see that Angela was clearly the leader. Both Julia and Ilsa looked at her with faces filled with admiration. Often he'd seen that same look in the eyes of investors he'd approached when he'd finished a particularly astute presentation. Angela had their rapt attention. Rafe couldn't help the proud smile that curved his lips.

When Angela finally left the restaurant, Rafe followed her at considerable distance since she knew his truck all too well. Once she turned onto Post Oak Lane, he knew she was headed for home.

Giving her time to park the car, walk Rebel and check

her mail, Rafe hid his truck two blocks away. Carrying his cellular phone with him, he walked to her front porch and rang the doorbell.

Hearing her coming down the stairs and then the sound of bare feet on the foyer floor, Rafe's heart immediately hammered against his chest. Rebel barked twice before Angela calmed him.

"It's probably UPS," she said to the dog.

Peeking out the side window, Angela stepped back from the door. Just the sight of him made her heart race.

"You should have called, Rafe."

"I can do that, too," he said shoving his cellular phone up to the window. "I'm not leaving this porch until you give me a chance, Angela. I'll stay here all night if I have to. Sooner or later you're going to have to hear me out."

"Later," she sighed. "I told you I'd see you at the closing."

Putting his hands frustratedly on his hips he said, "Fine. But before the closing, not after. In front of everyone…"

"Why are you doing this, Rafe?" she asked feeling a burning sob rise in her throat, and tears she believed she'd purged days ago.

"Let me in, Angela." He leaned up against the door. "Please."

Blinking to keep from crying, Angela was determined to meet him with a stoic face. She was at peace with her decision and she knew she was fine. The only problem was that she truly loved him. She would get over him in time, wouldn't she? Wasn't that what people always said about lost love? Time healed all wounds, didn't it?

With trembling hands, Angela unlocked the door.

Why couldn't he be less soulful-looking? Why couldn't he have turned into the hideous monster I've made him into these past days? Why can't he stop pulling my heart-strings?

Rafe's smile came from his eyes, not his lips. "Thanks," he said moving quickly into the room before she had a chance to slam the door in his face.

God, you look incredible. I've never seen you quite so content, so sure of yourself. I wish to heaven I could touch you. Maybe I could absorb some of your strength. "Just hear me out, Angela. That's all I ask."

"Okay," she replied politely, clasping her shaking hands behind her back. "Let's go into the living room," she offered, leading the way.

The scent of her perfume filled his nostrils, and watching the way she gracefully held her shoulders as she walked in front of him, Rafe wondered how he'd managed to live through this past week without her.

Gently placing his hand on her arm, he halted and turned her to face him. "I know what you're thinking, Angela."

"I doubt it," she said in what she hoped was a neutral voice, wondering if his eyes had always been this sincere.

"Because of what I said, you think I believe the baby's not mine."

"Is it mine?" The words spiraled across Angela's memory. For a while she'd been able to fool herself that they didn't sting when they slashed her heart. Now she realized they were torture no woman should ever endure. It wasn't easy being courageous under any circumstances, but Angela was the only person she could turn to for protection.

She stared back at him. "You believe I keep more than one lover. You believe I was dishonest. You believe I played games with you. Used you. Then tried to trap you into marriage."

Each of her biting accusations caused Rafe to flinch. It sounded a hundred times worse coming from her. "I don't think any of those things," he said earnestly.

Preparing herself to blast him with another round of accusations, Angela nearly didn't hear him, but she saw the pain at the edges of his eyes. "What?"

Placing his hands gently on her shoulders he began, "This misunderstanding is all my fault because of something that happened to me. Her name was Cheryl Hudson."

Stunned that Rafe had finally put a name to the heartache she'd sensed in him from the beginning, Angela replied, "Go on."

"I was in love with her..." he began his story. He told Angela the basic facts leaving out the parts that he knew would cause her consternation or hurt feelings. He told her that Cheryl had never wanted him or loved him. She had used him to get the things she wanted and when that wasn't enough, she began sleeping with his partner.

"Cheryl was carrying Paul's baby for three months before she told me about it. I told her that I wanted nothing more than to be a father and have a family. She didn't want any part of my dreams or to live at the ranch. After she left I tried to call Paul, but there was no answer on his phone. Then I discovered he'd disconnected his cellular phone. That's when I knew I was only beginning to learn the real truth. I realized they'd planned the embezzlement for quite some time. I went to the office that night and found Paul had cleaned out his desk. I've never heard from either one of them."

"And that's why you had to file bankruptcy?"

"Yes." He moved a step closer to her now that the burden of his confession was gone.

Angela stepped back. "Well, thank you for explaining

all this to me, Rafe. Now, if you don't mind, I'm very tired and I'd like to get some sleep. I have a busy day tomorrow.''

Stunned at her cavalier reply, he ground his jaw. ''Dammit, Angela, don't you see that I want nothing more than to be with you and care for you and our baby!''

She glanced away trying to avoid the pain in his eyes. She didn't want him to see hers either. ''I see nothing of the sort.''

''I can't believe this! Then tell me what you do see.''

Raising her tear-filled eyes to him she said, ''I don't want a man who is still in love with someone else.''

''I'm not! I swear...''

''Every time you made love to me, you were trying to purge your memories of her. I gave you everything I had and you carefully held yourself back. I was so stupid as to think that I could make you love me. Make you tell me that you loved me. Like you were some damn challenge. That was wrong of me and I admit it. I did all those things for you because I loved you. Sometimes when I was at the ranch with you, it was like I was living a dream. And in the end I discovered that's exactly what it was. A dream. A fantasy.''

''You're wrong, Angela. I'm real. Very real. I've been hurt, is all and I admit that I didn't say and do some of the things I should have.'' He pulled her close to him and though she was reluctant, he succeeded in drawing her into the circle of his arms.

Rafe lifted her chin with his forefinger. ''I love you with all my heart, Angela. I've never loved anyone in this world as much as I love you and I never will. My experience with Cheryl was fortunate in the end, because now I'm able to compare the false with the real. And you know what I've discovered? I know that true love isn't something that comes and goes. It's not offered up every other year, in case this time you're interested. You have to be wise enough to know true love when it happens. You are my true love.''

His thoughts tumbling through his head faster than he could speak, Rafe allowed his heart to flow freely. ''If you were to give up on me, on us, I know I'd never get over you, Angela. Maybe you could find someone else, but I don't really believe that. I'll never share what we've had together. Never.

''If you were truly honest with yourself, I think you'd admit that to me. Oh, you could find a guy who would be willing to marry you, raise our baby and be good to you. You deserve all that. But you can't tell me in a million years you'll ever feel about another man the way you feel about me. You'll never make love to anyone and feel as if you were one heart, one soul, the way you have with me. You were meant to be with me, Angela. You know how I know?''

She was crying huge tears, but she managed to ask, ''How?'' *Was it possible? He was voicing the very same feelings she'd had about their love. Was it possible that two people could think and be that much alike? Had she been wrong about him again? Was he the one true love she'd waited for?*

''Because the angels gave us this child you're carrying. On my life, I've always believed my life was charmed in some way. My grandparents believed that about themselves and they did live a great and wonderful life because they *expected* nothing but the best of themselves, for themselves. My parents were the same. This child is a sign to us, Angela, that we can't let our pride or past pains keep us from loving each other. Because when I'm with you, I'm the best I can be. I'd like to think you feel the same about me.''

Cautiously absorbing Rafe's words, Angela felt her joy being snarled with fear. ''I don't think I could stand it if you felt, even for a moment, that I was using the baby to trap you.''

''Does it look like I'm doing that?''

''Not now, it doesn't. But what about years from now?''

''I'll still be in love with you, Angela. It sounds to me that you're the one who's not so sure. It sounds as if you're planning our ending before we've begun.''

''I'm being careful,'' she replied still gazing into his eyes for flickers of falsehoods.

He shook his head. ''There's no reason to be,'' he said and leaned his face very close to hers. ''I've never told anyone this, but my mother was six months pregnant with me when they married.''

Angela nearly dropped her jaw. ''I don't believe you.''

''Why would I make it up?'' he reasoned.

''To trap me into marrying you!'' She'd barely gotten the words out when he chuckled and playfully kissed her bottom lip.

''The only reason I'd want to do that was because I wanted you to be my wife, wouldn't it?''

''Yes, but…''

Putting his finger on her lip to quiet her, he said, ''I love you with all my heart, Angela. The only thing I can tell you is that sometimes in life we have to take a chance. I'm willing to take one with you. You think I'll feel you trapped me. Maybe you'll feel trapped by me. Maybe we're both wrong. I'm willing to find out. Do you love me enough to marry me?''

His eyes had never been more sincere or trusting. As

he placed his lips next to hers and she felt her heart open once again to him, Angela knew she was making the right decision.

"I'll marry you, Rafe," she whispered between tender passionate kisses.

"You've made me the happiest man alive," he said lifting her into his arms and heading toward the staircase. "I intend to spend the rest of my life showing you..." he glanced down at her abdomen with gentle caring in his blue eyes, "that happiness isn't meant to be a dream."

* * * * *

Dear Reader,

This is my first book for Silhouette and many of you are meeting me for the first time. In my seventeen years of writing, I have always liked to surprise my readers by including recipes hidden in the story. Not only do my readers write to me about the stories, they often request my recipes. My recipes are family favorites, some going back to my childhood. These days I've doctored most of them with more spices and garlic and a lot less fat.

Since this story is set in Houston, my home, I thought this time I would share my favorite grilled veal chop recipe and with it, my garlic-cooked spinach. The key to this meal is to serve the two flavors together with some oven-browned potatoes because the blend of the rosemary on the veal chop and the garlic in the spinach will make your taste buds sing!

Also, I have been slowly learning about wines and will now include tastefully matched red wines. If you would like an autographed copy of Angela's Rosemary Veal Chop and Garlic Cooked Spinach please send a self-addressed stamped envelope to me at 5644 Westheimer, P.O. Box #110, Houston, Texas, 77056.

I read every one of your letters and believe me, your comments are invaluable. I'd love to hear your thoughts about Angela and Rafe. Write and tell me what you liked most, and what kind of stories you'd like to see from me in the future.

Thank you for your support and the next time you go to your bookstore, look for my MIRA book, *Tender Malice,* 3/98. I have great recipes in there as well!

Affectionately,
Catherine Lanigan

Turn the page for a sneak preview of

TENDER MALICE

by

Catherine Lanigan

coming in March 1998
only from

1

![section divider]

Austin, Texas
Christmas Eve

Karen faced death with her eyes open.

A menacing figure, dressed completely in black with a black wool ski mask covering all but his eyes, leaped out of the shadows of the parking garage of Dale Computers, Inc. and cocked back the hammer of a .357 Magnum.

The pounding of her feet against the concrete and the roar of her own breathing drowned out the sound of her assailant's voice as he chased her down the long aisles of cars.

"Stop!" The voice shattered the night and seemed to come at her from all sides making her feel as if she were surrounded.

Glancing back over her shoulder, Karen could no longer see the dark angel. He seemed to have disappeared. *I'm not ready to die!*

Thinking fast, Karen bolted left and up the ramp toward her car.

Wrong move, she thought as she realized the gunman had climbed up from the lower level and was coming toward her with the gun pointed directly at her.

Karen stopped in her tracks. Staring down the barrel of the steel gray gun, terror turned her blood to ice. Her head felt light. Colors became acute and surreal. Everything looked as if it had been outlined in black. She felt as if she were not even part of her body anymore and the strangest thoughts flitted through her mind.

As if her nervous system had completely shut down, she became numb. Suddenly, before her eyes, the gun turned a bloody red.

Had her heart stopped?

Her breath was stuck in her lungs. Her pulse thundered through her temples. She felt trapped, powerless. She was out of options. It was a terrifying sensation. Karen didn't like it one damn bit.

Squeezing the trigger, the dark angel smiled as the hammer moved forward. In that split second time froze.

Her father's face flashed across her mind. *Oh, Pop, I love you. Will I ever see you again?*

She smelled her assailant's fetid scent, whether from his breath or sweat, she couldn't tell. *Evil stinks.*

The hammer continued moving. Karen was stunned she was still alive. *I hate you! Do you know that? I'll never see Mastermind become reality. My life has been Mastermind. It's my genius not yours! You can't have it! No one can.*

"Die bitch!"

The words shot through Karen. And she stiffened. *Not a bullet. Just words.*

She was still alive. *A reprieve.*

Once the bullet was ejected from the barrel of the gun, Karen wouldn't have to think any longer about shattered dreams or time lost with her father.

She would be dead.

Like hell!

Defiance and anger ignited her. "No!"

Karen darted forward and threw an adrenaline-packed

punch to the gunman's midsection. He was caught off-guard, and the gun went off.

The shot missed.

She ran.

The dark angel crumbled at the waist, his hand wavering as he aimed the gun again.

"Son of a bitch!" Karen skidded on the smooth pavement. Behind her the gun fired again.

She felt a burning sensation erupt in her left arm and fell to the pavement.

I've been shot!

Get up! Get up! She scrambled to her feet, as he raced toward her, still doubled over at the waist.

He grabbed her ankle. His grip was strong, but not strong enough.

She screamed and kicked him in the jaw. Breaking free, she darted up the incline to the next level, where she'd parked her car.

The pain from the gunshot wound immobilized her left arm, making her fumble as she tried to get the keys out of her pocket.

Precious seconds went by as she struggled to get the key in the lock. But her good arm was shaking so much she dropped the keys. Stooping to retrieve them, she heard the gunman racing up the ramp.

With no time to think, Karen lunged toward the car, inserted the key and unlocked the door. Her fingers were turning ice cold again.

Christ! Not now!

Frantically, she turned the key. Nothing happened. Forcing herself to stay calm, she carefully eased the gas into the lines while sharply turning the key, which was the only

way to bring the old clunker to life. It was a trick she'd
learned when she'd bought the car a month ago.

Sorry day that was!

Finally, the engine turned over. But just as she put the car
in Reverse, the assailant's gloved hands shattered the window and grabbed Karen around the throat.

"God..."

He choked off her cry.

She flailed at him, but couldn't break his grip.

Twisting her body from one side to the other, she desperately gasped for air. She didn't know if she'd suffocate first
or choke from swallowing her tongue. *No oxygen. Can't
breathe. Can't fight.*

The world started going black like when she'd played
hide and seek with her father after dark.

Ollie, ollie, oxen free. I give up... Sorry, Pop.

Maybe it was the thought of her father. Maybe it was her
own irrepressible will. Whatever it was, before she lost consciousness, something made her press down on the accelerator with every ounce of strength she had left.

The car jerked backward and rammed into the car
parked behind it.

"Ahh!" The assailant shouted as his black-gloved hands
fell away from Karen's throat.

Grabbing the gear shift, Karen quickly put the car into
Drive. She hit the gas again, and the car lurched forward
dragging the gunman along. Using a wood-handled um-
brella that was on the seat next to her, she struck him just
above his wrists.

"Bitch!"

He dropped away from the speeding car like a heavy bag
of refuse.

Sucking in air, Karen felt her body come alive as she sped

down the ramp and out of the parking garage. She kept the accelerator pressed to the floor as she exited the Dale complex, sped along the frontage road and then merged quickly into the night traffic.

The twelve-year-old Cutlass Supreme barely chugged along in traffic. It was no match for the Porsches, BMWs and expensive Japanese cars that did zero to sixty in less than ten seconds.

"Next time, I'm buying foreign and expensive," she said half hysterically as she glanced in the rearview mirror. To her horror she saw the approaching headlights of a black Ferrari.

Dodging traffic, the Ferrari went from the far right lane to the far left lane scraping against the concrete construction barrier, sending glittering sparks into the dark night.

As it bore down on her, Karen struggled to keep ahead of the Ferrari. She swerved into the far right lane and bumped the side of a shiny new flatbed truck.

The cowboy driving it shook his fist at her. "Crazy broad!"

Desperate to escape the Ferrari, she ignored him. The Ferrari was merciless to other drivers on the highway. Ramming other cars until they gave way or moved to the shoulder, it gained on Karen at a frightening pace.

"Think fast, Karen," she said aloud as green exit signs flew past her.

The Ferrari was gaining.

She felt terror return.

He'd be on her bumper in seconds. He'd ram her just once and she'd sheer the concrete construction barricade. *I'm dead meat.*

What were her options?

Think, baby. Think.

Wheels squealing, Karen jerked her car off the highway onto the feeder.

The Ferrari followed.

Noticing that construction crews dominated all but one lane of the highway up ahead, Karen decided to stay on the feeder until the second entrance ramp. She'd go around the stop-and-go traffic that was accumulating from the mall in the next block and then re-enter the highway. Then she'd continue to the next exit, turn off, take the underpass and double back around, leading the Ferrari across town toward police headquarters.

Not the best of plans. But a plan.

Karen didn't check the rearview mirror so she didn't see a barricade being placed on the feeder exit she'd just driven through. Nor did she see the Ferrari smash through the barricade. But Karen did see another barricade going up right across the middle of the road ahead. Two construction workers wearing bright orange vests and holding flashlights were directing all the traffic to detour down a residential street. From what she could tell, the traffic was slower on the feeder than on the highway. If she exited the feeder and tried to race through a neighborhood on Christmas Eve with half of Austin on their way to night services and the other half heading to family gatherings, she could very well be the cause of injury, even death to innocent bystanders.

Karen's only chance was to cut across the grassy drainage ditch, go around the barrier then up to the highway, working her way around whatever construction there was.

Behind her, horns blared at the Ferrari as it snaked through traffic. Metal scraped metal.

Karen yanked on the steering wheel and pressed down on the accelerator. *I've only got one way out.*

Faulty suspension aside, the Cutlass shot across the rugged ditch and in seconds, the car was back on the highway.

The moment she saw the abandoned construction site, she realized the workers on the feeder had been finishing for the night when they'd put up the barricades. Bright orange barrels were lined up along both sides of the highway. Yellow-and-black-striped barricades topped with flashing yellow lights stood guard at what looked like the end of the earth.

The Cutlass engine roared as she pushed it to the limit.

The Ferrari roared more fiercely as it gained on her.

Stupid! Stupid! Stupid!

Not once during her flight from the complex, not once as she watched the Ferrari race toward her had she remembered reading about the collapsed section of highway on this bridge. Because it was a route she seldom took, she'd paid no attention.

Now she remembered *everything*.

Kisses. Coercion. Lies. Promises. Fear. Hope. Making love. Being in love.

They were the threads of her life for the past year, now the tapestry was finally woven.

Too late!

The Cutlass hit the barricade. Splintered wood shot through the air.

She jammed on the brakes with both feet, and the Cutlass started to spin.

Ollie, ollie, oxen free. Oh, Pop...

Through the darkness she made out the edge of the crumbled highway and the abyss beyond.

This time when she faced death, it didn't matter if her eyes were open or shut. Her life flashed through her mind.

And her heart broke.

She thought of the man who killed her. The man she loved.

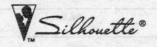

Take 4 bestselling love stories FREE

Plus get a FREE surprise gift!

Special Limited-time Offer

Mail to Silhouette Reader Service™

3010 Walden Avenue
P.O. Box 1867
Buffalo, N.Y. 14240-1867

YES! Please send me 4 free Silhouette Desire® novels and my free surprise gift. Then send me 6 brand-new novels every month, which I will receive months before they appear in bookstores. Bill me at the low price of $3.12 each plus 25¢ delivery and applicable sales tax, if any.* That's the complete price and a savings of over 10% off the cover prices—quite a bargain! I understand that accepting the books and gift places me under no obligation ever to buy any books. I can always return a shipment and cancel at any time. Even if I never buy another book from Silhouette, the 4 free books and the surprise gift are mine to keep forever.

225 SEN CF2R

Name	(PLEASE PRINT)	
Address	Apt. No.	
City	State	Zip

This offer is limited to one order per household and not valid to present Silhouette Desire® subscribers. *Terms and prices are subject to change without notice. Sales tax applicable in N.Y.

UDES-696

©1990 Harlequin Enterprises Limited

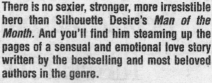

**Make a Valentine's date
for the premiere of**

◆ **HARLEQUIN**® **Movies**

starting February 14, 1998 with

Debbie Macomber's

This Matter of

Marriage

on **themovie channel** tmc

Just tune in to **The Movie Channel** the **second Saturday night** of every month at 9:00 p.m. EST to join us, and be swept away by the sheer thrill of romance brought to life. Watch for details of upcoming movies—in books, in your television viewing guide and in stores.

If you are not currently a subscriber to The Movie Channel, simply call your local cable or satellite provider for more details. Call today, and don't miss out on the romance!

*100% pure movies.
100% pure fun.*

◆ HARLEQUIN™

Makes any time special.™

Return to the Towers!

In March
New York Times bestselling author

NORA ROBERTS

brings us to the Calhouns' fabulous
Maine coast mansion and reveals the
tragic secrets hidden there for generations.

For all his degrees, Professor Max Quartermain has a
lot to learn about love—and luscious Lilah Calhoun is
just the woman to teach him. Ex-cop Holt Bradford is
as prickly as a thornbush—until Suzanna Calhoun's
special touch makes love blossom in his heart.
And all of them are caught in the race to solve
the generations-old mystery of a priceless
lost necklace...and a timeless love.

Lilah and Suzanna
THE
Calhoun Women

**A special 2-in-1 edition containing
FOR THE LOVE OF LILAH and
SUZANNA'S SURRENDER**

Available at your favorite retail outlet.

Angela stood her ground as she waited for his answer. That one tiny word had put him on the hot seat and they both knew it. She was going to get what she wanted; the truth.

Rafe actually trembled as he opened his mouth to speak. "Because if you stay, I *will* take you. Not here, but upstairs in my ancestors' bed. I'll make love to you all night and probably most of tomorrow, because when it comes to you, Angela, I lose all reason. One kiss isn't enough for me. You look at me with those deep brown eyes and I feel as if I can't sink myself far enough into you."

He clamped his hands on both sides of her face and peered into her eyes. "You make me crazy, Angela Morton. Crazier than I ever want to be. It's safe for both of us if you leave. We can tell ourselves we had a great fling. Then it'll be over."

"But you don't want it to be over, do you, Rafe?"

Slamming at breakneck speed against his chest, Rafe's heart recreated an internal inferno. "Not tonight, I don't."

"And tomorrow?" she baited him.

"Then either. I feel as if I could make love to you for months on end. We both know I'd get my fill sooner or later."

"Would you?"

"I always have before. Then you'll go away." He paused. "Like I said, it's easier for you to leave now."

Though her lips trembled at the very thought of losing him, she found the courage to say, "I'll take my chances."

"You're a fool, Angela," he warned.

"I've been accused of that before," she said slipping her arms around him once again.

Unable to hold himself back any longer, Rafe slanted